RUNNING
AWAY
FOR
BEGINNERS

RUNNING AWAY FOR BEGINNERS

MARK ILLIS

SCHOLASTIC

Published in the UK by Scholastic, 2024
1 London Bridge, London, SE1 9BG
Scholastic Ireland, 89E Lagan Road, Dublin Industrial Estate,
Glasnevin, Dublin, D11 HP5F

ISBN 978 0702 32993 7

A CIP catalogue record for this book
is available from the British Library.

Printed and bound in Great Britain by
Clays Ltd, Elcograf S.p.A
Paper made from wood grown in sustainable forests
and other controlled sources.

1 3 5 7 9 10 8 6 4 2

www.scholastic.co.uk

To Alan, Jacqui and Ginny, again

THURSDAY

ONE

I was up on the roof of the shed while my parents were indoors talking about me dying. Lying flat, eyes closed, soaking up sun like my mate Barney's iguana. It mostly sits under a heat lamp and ignores me when I go over there, but sometimes it looks right at me and sneers and hisses. (I might be imagining the sneer.)

"You're on the roof!"

OK, that was like magic. I'd been thinking about Barney, and now here he was. Barney: short hair, round face, big smile, looking up at me and stating the obvious, which is something he's good at.

"Oh yeah," I said, lifting myself up on my elbows and putting on a surprised face. "So I am."

Barney snorted. "Muppet."

He went round the back of the shed where the garden

slopes up a bit, so you can climb on to the roof easily via the compost bin.

"Hey," he said, as he slithered down and joined me.

"Hey back," I said, smiling. It was only when he'd showed up that I realized I'd been feeling lonely. "Did you see my parents?" I asked him.

"No," he said. "I came straight to the garden. Knew you'd be out here."

His hands were pressed flat against the rough, black surface. He didn't much like it on the roof, always said he was afraid he was going to roll right off. Barney's not keen on anything dangerous. He says that's just sensible, which is fair enough.

"How'd it go then?" he asked.

I didn't answer. Because it couldn't have gone much worse.

On the way back from the hospital earlier, Mum kept asking me how I felt. It was a bit irritating, because I didn't know what to say to her. I mean, I felt bad, obviously, but it was all too big to think about properly.

Barney had come straight from school, which was nice of him. He's my best friend – or my best friend who's a boy. Suravi's my best friend who's a girl, and she's great, in a slightly scary sort of way.

There are two big things to know about Suravi: first, she reckons she's always right about everything. For instance, she saw me when we were both in Year 3, at

4

Hazelwood Primary, messing about with flour and grated cheese, making cheese muffins. She paired up with me out of nowhere and said we were going to be friends. And she was right about that.

The second big thing is more difficult. She usually comes as a double act with Maika. And the problem with Maika is that I hate her because of the thing that happened between us last year. It's impossible to forget, partly because I still have a scar.

"You're on the roof!"

OK, this was getting spooky now. Every time I thought of someone, they showed up. Suravi was on the lawn, her face tipped up towards me, shielding her eyes, her long hair in a long braid. She's short, but she's loud. You always know she's there.

I looked around suspiciously. No sign of Maika. Good.

"I know I am!" I shouted.

Suravi went round the back, climbed up on the compost bin, came slithering down the roof and sat beside me and Barney. She leant back on her elbows, her knees pointing at the sky.

"So how'd it go?" she said.

"I just asked him that," Barney told her.

Suravi nodded impatiently. "And what did he say?"

"Nothing yet," said Barney.

And then they both looked at me, waiting.

It was September, and it smelled of autumn in the

garden: cut grass and smoke from someone burning leaves two doors down. The low sun was all dazzly. I scratched at the roofing felt, picking it with my fingernail. Barney and Suravi were still looking at me, waiting for me to say something. They knew I'd had X-rays and a CT scan and then a biopsy which involved an operation on my shoulder. Today was the day the doctor had finally told me and my parents what was going on.

I was still lying on my back. I pushed my long hair out of my eyes and glanced at Barney and Suravi, who were sitting up now and looking down at me. I had to screw up my eyes because the sun was too bright, so I closed them.

"Turns out I've got cancer," I said.

Barney made a sound which was somewhere between a sigh and a gasp. Suravi looked like she'd just bitten into something sour. And then I had to explain it for them. It's difficult explaining personal stuff like this because it's personal, and everyone's embarrassed, and no one really knows what to do with their faces. They're sorry, and they feel like they have to say they're sorry, but what am I supposed to say to that? "I'm sorry you're sorry"? "I'm sorry too"? If you're not careful, every conversation will be dripping with sorrys and self-consciousness and embarrassment. And no one wants that.

So I got all "clear and step-by-step", like Mr Locke, our maths teacher, always wants us to be. I didn't bother to say "Osteosarcoma", which sounds like a creature from

Star Wars. (*The Osteosarcoma rose from the swamp, its yellow eyes gleaming, and a tentacle whipped out and wrapped itself around Luke Skywalker's ankle…*) If I'd used that word, I'd have had to explain it, and I wasn't sure I could do that. I just told them there was a treatment plan, and I said there were three options; three things that could happen next:

1. The treatment might be pretty nasty, but it would work, and everything would be OK.
2. The treatment wouldn't work so well, and they'd have to do what the doctor had called "radical surgery". Which wouldn't be OK.

Actually, I didn't mention Option Three, because I didn't want to think about it. At all. I mean I'm an optimist, mostly, so why would I think about Option Three? Option Three made me feel like I was a little kid at the top of The Big One at Blackpool Pleasure Beach, about to plunge down, and I was looking at my dad for reassurance but my dad was as scared as I was. Anyway, I didn't need to mention Option Three because we all knew it existed. It was squatting inside my head like a big, poisonous toad.

"What's 'radical surgery'?" Suravi said.

"Don't want to talk about it," I told her.

"OK, but what's going to happen?" Barney said, his voice straying a little higher in pitch.

I know this is weird, but I sometimes think of a teddy bear when I think of Barney. He's not furry, but he's short and stocky, and he has a round smiley face and a reassuring friendly attitude which I think is the sort of attitude a teddy bear would have. I haven't told him this because I doubt that he actually *wants* to be perceived as a teddy bear.

"Chemotherapy starts in a week," I said, "so I'll be on drugs to kill the thing. The tumour." I closed my eyes again. The whole conversation seemed to be easier with my eyes closed. "And then after that, surgery, and then more chemo."

"Sucks," Suravi said, sounding like she wanted to hit something. Suravi has a reputation for hitting things. "So, what you gonna do for a week?"

I tapped the roof with my fingernails. When I spoke, my voice came out clipped and frustrated. "Mum and Dad want me to go to school. Like nothing's happened."

When my parents had told me that, I'd nodded without really thinking about it, but now when I said it out loud it sounded ridiculous. It was actually really irritating. We'd only just started Year 11 at Rudding High, and GCSEs were just around the corner, so my parents thought it was important to try to live an ordinary life. As much as possible. "Socially and academically, we think it's for the best, sweetheart," Mum had said. "Trust me."

"Well, that's rubbish," Suravi snorted. It sounded a bit like she was having a go at my mum and dad, but that didn't seem to bother her. She never thinks before she speaks and, like I said, she reckons she's always right; doesn't matter whether she's talking about a maths question or a TV show or her friend's life.

And in this case, she *was* right, so it didn't bother me either, but I didn't say anything. Because I didn't feel like saying anything. I was pleased Barney and Suravi were there, because they're my best friends and I liked having their support, but at the same time, I didn't actually feel like talking to them. Like I said, the whole thing was too big to think about.

No one spoke for a while. Silence, except for the fluty whistle of a bird and a bee buzzing lazily somewhere near my ear. Beneath the aroma of cut grass and the smoke, I could smell something damp and rotting in the compost.

Barney often stops talking when Suravi's around, which is fair enough because she takes up a lot of space. He has this way of just quietly looking at her. I'm pretty sure he likes her.

Anyway, after about ten seconds of me lying there with my eyes closed and no one saying anything, Barney spoke. And he said pretty much the very last thing I expected him to say.

"We could run away," he murmured, almost like he was hoping we wouldn't hear.

Well, that came out of nowhere.

I opened my eyes.

"Yeah, *great* idea," I said sarcastically, although, even then, the first time it was mentioned, I felt a jolt of excitement. For a moment, I imagined walking away from my life, leaving everything behind.

How good would that be?

I dismissed the idea pretty quickly, because it was just a fantasy. Obviously. Barney made a hurt little "humph" noise, and Suravi didn't say anything, just stared off in the distance, like she was thinking about it.

"I mean it's just not…" I started. And then I hesitated. What was it just not? "It's not even possible."

"Of course it's *possible*," Suravi said.

We were quiet again. Apparently, they were genuinely thinking about running away. Which was obviously never going to happen. I was a bit irritated to be honest, because I had a huge real-life problem, and my friends were thinking about a silly, impossible response to it.

Silence again. "My tea's probably ready," I said eventually.

"You're in school tomorrow, right?" Suravi said. "We'll see you then?"

I nodded. "Sure."

Barney said, "Bye," and there was definitely a bit of an atmosphere. He sounded like he was still annoyed with me, and Suravi seemed like her mind was elsewhere.

"Thanks for coming!" I said, upbeat and friendly, not wanting to fall out with them.

10

And that's where it all started. From that point onwards, Barney's idea was floating around us like a big red balloon, impossible to ignore. *Run away. Leave everything, including cancer, behind.* It was completely ridiculous. It was definitely never going to happen.

But Suravi had said it was possible, and the thing about Suravi is, she's always right.

TWO

Chicken Kiev from the supermarket, with a small mountain of creamy mashed potato and a load of peas. When I was about ten, I told Mum and Dad it was my favourite meal so it always gets rolled out when anything special is happening. I don't mind it, but, you know, I'm not ten any more. They must have planned it for tonight so they could either celebrate good news or try and make up for bad news. *OK, you've got cancer, but look – chicken Kiev!*

"It hasn't spread," Mum was saying, chopping the table with the side of her hand. "And that's a very good thing."

She was staring at me in that direct, serious way she sometimes does. There were big dark bags under her crinkly eyes and her face was pale, like she hadn't slept, which was probably my fault.

Dad nodded. "That means it's all in one place," he said. "They blitz it with their amazing drugs, they kill it."

12

He was staring at me too, eyebrows knitted as if I'd done something wrong. His fingers tapped on his cheekbone.

I nodded back at him. "Thanks," I said, putting a forkful of garlicky chicken in my mouth, "for this."

"Hey," said Dad, "of course."

"It's my favourite meal too," said Mum.

"And there's Bakewell tart and ice cream for afters," added Dad.

Which used to be my favourite pudding and, actually, still is. They were staring at me and smiling now, their lips tight, their eyes worried, and I suddenly felt like crying because they were being so nice. Mum must have seen my lip tremble because she put her hand on mine and squeezed it.

"We're going to get through this, sweetheart," she said fiercely, and then I was crying a bit (and, awkwardly, still chewing) and they were both hugging me and probably crying too. Which is why it's better not to talk about it. When you talk about it, it turns out you get this whole big crying and hugging mid-meal thing going on, which is probably really bad for digestion.

This was a good reason to not run away: the last thing I wanted to do was make this any worse for my parents. Mum works at a university. Not teaching; something involving "personnel". I don't know. Dad used to work at a bank but got made redundant and now he's a bit in and out of work. He volunteers in a charity shop and does

13

some book-keeping for people. Apparently, we're going to move house soon – Mum says it's because the house is too big, but really it's because we've been short of money since Dad lost his job. It doesn't seem like it's much fun being them, to be honest.

Anyway, the point is, there's all the usual things about screen-time and bedtime and nagging about mess and homework and going out more and going out less and everything else, but for the most part, they're a pretty decent mum and dad. For instance, Mum's into Marvel movies just as much as I am. We used to go to the cinema with the big seats that tip backwards and have a footrest, and we'd get a giant tub of popcorn, and she'd lean over to me just before the film started and say, "I'm so excited!" which was a bit embarrassing, but also nice. I go with my mates these days, but Mum and I still watch them at home sometimes. We don't have popcorn, but Dad bakes chocolate chip cookies from his mum's recipe. He reckons they're the best chocolate chip cookies in the world, which obviously they aren't, but still.

So, yeah, they're OK parents. And running away would be really mean. Unthinkable.

"Right," Mum said, "let's talk about next week. We think we should keep it basically routine, like we told you before. There's a nurse we're all going to meet on Wednesday after school, and treatment starts on Friday, but until then, me and Dad think it should be about life

14

carrying on – and that includes school. Let's just try to have an ordinary week." She looked at Dad. Her voice was a bit wobbly. "Carry on as normal! Right?"

"Right," he said, nodding, straightening his knife and fork on his empty plate. "We think we should keep everything … you know …" – he was still nodding – "normal." He pointed at me. "But what do you think, buddy?"

I stared at them, anger suddenly bubbling inside me. *What do I think?*

When we were walking out of the hospital, I saw some people chatting and laughing about something, and I felt like stopping and saying to them, "Don't you know what's just happened?" It didn't seem fair that for everyone except me the world was exactly the same as it had always been. How could they not notice that everything had changed?

"Normal?" I said finally. My voice was quiet, but it was trembling a bit. "Carry on as normal? Seriously?"

"Wait—" Mum said.

But I didn't wait. "Could anything be *less* normal than it is right now?" I asked, my voice getting louder and cracking a bit.

They both started talking at once.

"No, of course—" Mum said.

"Yeah, we understand—" Dad said.

"No, you don't!" I shouted. And I walked out of the

15

room. I stood up, walked out, and then ran up the stairs. I just didn't want to be there any more.

About twenty minutes later, I was sat on my bed watching Netflix on my phone when there was a knock at my door. Mum came in with a dish of Bakewell tart and ice cream. She sat next to me and put an arm round me, which made eating the tart awkward, but I didn't tell her to stop. We just sat there like that for a bit, neither of us saying anything, me eating my favourite pudding but not enjoying it at all.

"This is so hard," she told me finally. "I'm so sorry this is happening to you."

I nodded. I was glad my mouth was full so I couldn't speak.

"It's a horrible situation," she continued, "and it's scary. Can you tell me what you're thinking, sweetheart? What you're feeling?"

It was the same question she'd kept asking on the way back from the hospital. I tried to work it out: I was still angry, and I was scared of course, but "scared" didn't really cover it. My whole understanding of what it meant to be alive had shifted, so I felt confused and small. And I was lonely too. I mean, my mum was right there with her arm round me, but I was lonely because this was happening to me, just me, and no one else could really understand. But all of that felt too painful and complicated to put into words. It was still too big to think about.

So I just shrugged.

She waited a moment for anything more and then she kissed the side of my head. "It's going to take a while to get used to this. For you, and for me, and your dad too. There's a lot of change coming your way. A lot. So that's why we think, I guess …" – she sighed and moved back a bit, lifting her hands, palms outwards – "don't rush it. Live your life as usual for now, and then, when the change comes, we'll deal with it together. Does that make sense?"

No. It feels like you're trying to control me.

I didn't say that. I didn't want an argument. I swallowed the last of my Bakewell tart and mumbled, "OK."

Mum nodded. "Life carries on," she told me. "The three of us, your friends, school. Me and your dad want all of that to be a sort of reliable constant – something that doesn't change."

"Sure," I said flatly.

She sighed again and stood up. I realized I'd said exactly two words to her so I tried some more as I gave her my empty dish. "Thanks for this," I said. "Really nice."

She held my cheeks and kissed my forehead. "*You're* really nice," she said.

I rolled my eyes.

She laughed and closed my door behind her. I started getting ready for bed, but I sat down on my duvet again with my T-shirt in my hand. My right shoulder ached. There was a small scar on it from the biopsy, and a small

17

bump, which was the thing. The tumour. I'm left-handed, which is probably just as well. I rubbed it gently.

There was a party at Jordan's on Saturday which I'd been looking forward to, but I didn't fancy it now. I didn't know what I wanted to do with my weekend. Maybe a film to take my mind off stuff. Next week there were trials for the football team, but there probably wasn't much point in putting myself up for that. It felt like there wasn't much point in anything, really.

I was addicted to the Netflix show I'd been watching when Mum came in. It involved zombies taking over the earth. And the thing is, I'd noticed that in the show the parents didn't try to "carry on as normal", didn't try to give their kids a "reliable constant". In fact, they taught them how to use special crossbows that fired flaming arrows at the zombies. I didn't want a special crossbow, I knew that wasn't going to help, but I didn't want to pretend nothing had changed either.

I weighed my choices in my mind: on the one hand there was what my parents wanted, which made no sense at all since my life had completely changed, and on the other hand there was Barney's idea, running away, which was ridiculous. *Brilliant.* It's great how the world opens up for you when you're fifteen.

FRIDAY

THREE

Mr Hoffman smiled at me in the corridor. He *smiled* at me! Mr Hoffman never smiles at anyone; it literally never happens. Then, during registration, Mrs Wells sat me down at her desk with her stern face on, as if she was about to tell me I'd let myself down very badly and I was in detention for the rest of my life.

"This is a very difficult time for you, Jasper." Her voice was low, her hands were clasped, and after a moment I realized it wasn't her stern face – it was meant to be a concerned face. The two are quite similar. Her forehead was wrinkled as if she was thinking hard about what she was saying. "Very difficult," she repeated. "But I want you to know that I'm here to support you, and we all want to stand with you ... at this very difficult time."

Yes, by the way, it's Jasper. I was named after my granddad. I realize it makes me sound like someone in a book written about two hundred years ago, probably the bad guy, probably with a moustache and a top hat, but what can I do about it? I can't shorten it to Jas because that sounds like some kind of sparkly doll's name.

I nodded at Mrs Wells and glanced over at Barney, who was grinning at me. He pulled a face – eyes wide, mouth wide open – like someone screaming in a horror film. That didn't help.

"Thanks," I muttered.

And I meant it, because it was nice of Mrs Wells. But like I said before, everyone's embarrassed, everyone's sorry, and no one knows what to do with their faces. I'd told Barney and Suravi that they weren't allowed to mention me being sick to anyone else. Obviously, the teachers all knew, and obviously everyone else would know sooner or later, but I wanted to keep it secret as long as I could. But with Mr Hoffman smiling, Mrs Wells with her concerned face, Barney with his horror-film face (which admittedly was quite funny), it was still really awkward and really embarrassing.

And not at all normal.

It didn't get any better after that. In maths we had a lesson on probability: how likely it was you'd roll a particular set of numbers with three dice. It was actually quite interesting, but it made me start thinking about Options One, Two and Three. How likely was each of those outcomes for me? When I thought about that, I felt like I had some sort of spiky lump in my chest, so I stopped listening to Mr Locke and stared out of the window instead. I'm pretty sure he knew I wasn't paying attention but he didn't say anything. When the bell went he set homework and as I was leaving he said, "Just do your best, Jasper."

In physics, Miss Ahmed asked me a question about electromagnetic radiation. She might as well have been speaking Russian. I said I didn't understand. She's one of those teachers who's usually really sarcastic and seems to enjoy making you feel small, but she just smiled, said, "Not to worry," and moved on to someone else.

So Mr Hoffman, Mrs Wells, Mr Locke and Miss Ahmed definitely hadn't got the memo about carrying on as if nothing had happened. It felt like they were shouting, "We know you've got cancer!" So if they couldn't be normal, why should I be? The whole idea, like I said, made no sense. It felt like I was carrying a huge flashing sign around saying:

CARRY ON AS NORMAL!

Which made it completely impossible to carry on as normal.

It was a relief when it was finally time for lunch. I sat down at my table with my tray. I had a spicy chicken wrap and a spongey thing with custard. I don't even like wraps, there's always too much wrap and not enough other stuff, especially in the corners, and I prefer ice cream to custard. I was picking the wrap up and sniffing it suspiciously when I saw Joe Hancock talking to Barney over by the counter. It didn't look very friendly.

"What was that about?" I asked when Barney finally sat down next to me.

He scooped up a forkful of mash and beans. "Nothing," he said.

I didn't believe him and I was about to say something, but he spoke first: "Why would anyone make mash when you can make chips?"

Suravi sat down opposite me. "You all right?" she asked.

"No, I'm not," Barney told her. "I don't like mash."

Suravi huffed out a sigh. "Not you. Him." She pointed at me with her knife.

I gave her a look. The secrecy around me being sick wasn't ideal because it made me feel like I was in a little bubble, separate from my other friends. Still, I preferred it this way. Far less awkwardness and embarrassment.

Suravi was saving a seat for Maika, because Maika was doing choir practice apparently. But this whole big swarm of Year 13 girls descended, and one of them grabbed the seat she was saving, scraping it across the floor. Suravi stood up and grabbed it back.

"This one's taken," she said.

I didn't know the Year 13 girl's name, but she looked a

bit like a Disney princess – big eyes and shiny blonde hair in a ponytail which hung perfectly between her shoulder-blades. Mind you, she was also wearing football kit and she was chewing gum.

"Wait," she said. Then she looked hard at the empty chair like maybe she was missing something. "Nope, pretty sure no one's sitting here" – all her friends laughed – "so it's not taken, is it?"

She tried to yank it out of Suravi's hand.

Suravi's short, like I said, she's got a pointy chin, and with her braid bouncing on her back she looks cute and friendly. People who don't know her think she's sweet. She's not sweet. She yanked the chair back again.

"Hey," I said, "don't—"

"Suravi—" Barney said at the same time.

We could both see the warning signs. Suravi's nostrils were flaring, her lips were pulling back, her teeth gritting. She has a real problem with her temper.

The Year 13 girl let go of the chair, but only so she could put her finger right in Suravi's face. She smiled in a nasty way. "What's your name? Subaru? Listen to your little friends, Subaru," she said.

So Suravi picked up the chair and threw it.

By now Miss Alam had spotted that something was going on and was coming over. And just to be completely clear, Suravi did *not* throw the chair at Miss Alam. She didn't even throw it at the Disney princess. Suravi just gets

25

angry and frustrated, like the Incredible Hulk, only less green. So she was actually throwing the chair away, as if she was saying, *Fine, neither of us can have it!*

But it did hit Miss Alam.

Miss Alam staggered back and fell into someone's mashed potato. The chair clattered on to the floor with a sound like a thrash metal band tuning up.

The whole canteen went silent.

Then Miss Alam straightened up slowly, wiping mashed potato off her elbow. She glared at Suravi with eyes like laser beams.

Suravi swallowed.

Disney princess smirked.

I wasn't even directly involved, but my skin was prickling and my cheeks were going red. I saw Maika arriving, looking at Miss Alam, looking at Suravi, trying to work out what was going on as Suravi and the princess were hauled off. Barney was just sitting there with beans falling from his fork. I had a sudden, urgent wish that we were all still in Year 7, or back at Hazelwood Primary, when life had been a whole lot simpler. I stood up.

"What you doing?" asked Barney.

"Going home," I said.

Because the awkwardness and embarrassment around carrying on as normal, and now the drama with Suravi, meant that this was all too much. I didn't have space for it inside my head, or inside my chest. Those bits of me were too full with other stuff: with that spiky lump, and with Options One, Two and also Three.

So I picked up my bag and went home.

I ate a slice of toast with peanut butter and jam because I'd never finished my lunch. Then I lay on my bed and watched that zombie show on my phone for a bit. I'd already binged seven episodes and the big end-of-season finale was coming, but I couldn't focus on it at all. So I gave up and went into the garden. I was back on the roof of the shed when they all turned up. All of them. Barney and Suravi. And Maika. She was tall and slim, in a sleeveless T-shirt. She looked great – athletic, like she was walking into a stadium about to throw a javelin or something, but she was frowning under her boyish blonde haircut, as if somehow I'd done something to annoy her before I'd even said a word.

"No," I said. "No way. What is she doing here?"

"Shut up!" said Suravi.

"I don't want her in my garden!" I said. Which, to be honest, sounded lame even to me.

"I asked her to come," Suravi said.

"I'm sorry you've got cancer," Maika muttered.

I sighed. All I wanted was a bit of control over my own life. Why was that so hard?

"I mean," I said, "I feel like what I want should get priority here. What with, you know, everything."

Maika shrugged. She glanced at Suravi, then looked at me. "I'll go," she said.

And then I felt like the bad guy, which seemed completely unfair. Maika was walking away, Suravi was glaring at me, even Barney looked a bit sad. And I was sad too, to be honest, because I hadn't always hated Maika. And I didn't actually want to be a horrible person.

"Wait," I said. "No. It's fine."

It wasn't fine, not really, but Maika staying in the garden seemed like the least bad option. She hesitated, looking up at me on the roof, then came back, and they all climbed up with me.

"So what happened?" I was looking at Suravi. "With Miss Alam."

Barney shook his head. "Oh my God! You can't throw chairs at teachers."

"I didn't!" Suravi protested. "I threw a chair which accidentally hit a teacher."

"Oh, fair enough." I nodded. "Yeah, that's completely different. She probably said that was fine, did she?"

Suravi shrugged. "It's not a big deal."

I saw her and Maika exchange a look when she said that, and I might have asked more, but then Barney turned to me. "How you feeling, though?" His smiley face looked more worried than usual. "You all right? I mean, you're not, but you know what I mean."

"OK," I said. "I've been thinking about it."

They all stared at me. "Thinking about what?" asked Barney.

"Running away?" said Suravi.

I'd been thinking about it a lot. It wasn't really something I could not think about. My thoughts bumped around in my head, making it hard to do maths, or sleep, or function. School was the very last place I wanted to be. And my parents were telling me to **CARRY ON AS NORMAL!** but that just felt wrong and also impossible. I was going to be sixteen next year, which meant I was basically an adult, and I didn't want parents and teachers and doctors all ordering me around.

So I needed to leave school and my parents and my whole ordinary life behind.

And cancer. I wanted to leave that behind too.

Because Options Two and Three were right here, they were in my garden and in my house, and in the hospital a few miles down the road. So, obviously, I wanted to be somewhere else, miles and miles away. Obviously!

I lifted myself up on my elbows and looked at them.

"I want to run away," I told them. "I don't want to be here any more. I want to be a missing person." I shrugged and sighed. "Problem is, I don't see how it's possible."

Suravi stared at me, all serious. "Told you before," she said quietly and slowly, like she was considering it while she was saying it. "It's definitely possible. And we can help you do it."

Just like that. I hid my surprise and looked at Maika and

Barney. Maika nodded. She seemed to think she was involved in this too, which she definitely wasn't. Barney's closed lips slid sideways. I thought he was biting the inside of his cheek, and maybe wishing he'd never suggested it in the first place. But he nodded too. They were *much* more serious about this than I'd expected. In fact, it was as if the idea of running away had been in their heads already, before I even got ill.

"OK," I said. "I didn't expect this. How come you're all totally up for running away with me?"

"Because we're your mates, you fool," Suravi said, as if it was the most obvious thing in the world.

"These last few weeks you've been having X-rays and scans, and then that operation on your shoulder, and we've been worried about you," Barney said, his voice getting more high-pitched and anxious.

Maika didn't say anything, but she nodded again.

"So we want to help you do whatever you need to do," Suravi said firmly. "Simple."

"Where would you go, if you could go anywhere?" asked Barney. "I'd go to Las Vegas!" he continued, not giving me a chance to answer. "I've always wanted to go to a casino, and they've got this hotel with an actual theme park attached, so that would be perfect."

"If we're going to America," Suravi said, "I want to go to New York."

"Yeah," Barney said, agreeing with her almost too quickly. "New York would be good too."

I laughed. "Yes, please," I said. "I want to go to Las Vegas *and* New York, and also I went to Spain last year and that was nice, but has anyone got about a thousand quid for flights? No? Probably not going to happen then."

No one said anything for a bit.

"Edinburgh!" Suravi shouted suddenly. She quite often shouts words when it isn't entirely necessary. "If we're serious about this, then we share our money, find some scuzzy, cheap place, get jobs…"

I saw Barney blink. He definitely wasn't up for that. It didn't sound too good to me either, to be honest.

"Might be better not being in a city," Barney said slowly. "My family went to Ullswater last summer. It's one of the lakes." We were all waiting for the "but". With Barney there was usually a sad little "but" after what should have been a nice thing. "But it rained," he finished.

As we talked, the ideas got more viable. I got out my phone and wrote down the places we came up with. Pretty soon we had a list:

PLACES WE COULD GO

1. Edinburgh
2. Ullswater
3. Whitby
4. London

"And York," said Maika, looking over my shoulder. She sounded irritated. She pretty much always sounds irritated around me. (Maika's not even her real name, it's Maia, but she doesn't like it. I don't blame her. It's one of those names you can spell pretty much however you want.)

If we actually went anywhere, there was no way she was coming along, but I added York to avoid an argument, thinking, *Not going to happen*.

"Liverpool," Suravi said. "Put Liverpool on the list. I've never been there."

"Oh, how about Alton Towers?" Barney actually had his hand up. "But I bet there'd be huge queues for everything."

"All right, all right!" I banged the roof. "You're just saying names now."

We live in a little town between Leeds and Manchester, basically right in the middle of the country only up a bit, so the places we'd thought of were in the North, except for maybe Alton Towers. I didn't know where that was. And London.

I stared at the list. They were all more realistic than Las Vegas, New York or Spain, but it was pretty obvious that the four of us had different ideas about running away. I didn't want to live in some scuzzy place and get a job. I wanted to be somewhere else, and I was surprised that my friends did too, but I still didn't really know what "running away" actually meant. The whole concept felt vague and unlikely, like a ridiculous thing Barney had said, that we'd talk about, but that we'd never actually do.

I stared at the words on my phone.

Frustrated, I closed my eyes.

And then I pictured a little village by the sea that I only partially remembered, and two words arrived in my head in big, flashing capitals:

UNCLE UNIVERSE

And that's when everything changed. That's when the whole fuzzy, out-of-focus picture of running away suddenly resolved into sharply outlined, high-definition clarity. A plan emerged, and it wasn't a ridiculous plan. It was rational. Mostly.

I knew where I could go, and I knew why I wanted to go there.

I opened my eyes and stared at my phone for a few more seconds, controlling my excitement, while I tried to work out what to say to my friends. The problem now was how to change this whole discussion into a real thing. And I knew how to do that.

It involved lying to them.

"Right, here's the plan," I said, all casual. "We don't run away, not this time. This time is just, like, a practice. It's running away for beginners. So, we go away for the weekend. We leave tomorrow, Saturday, then we come back home on Sunday evening in time for school on Monday."

Suravi tutted. "Really?"

I knew Suravi would be the problem. She seemed to have a pretty clear vision in her head of running away properly.

I nodded at her. "Really."

Maika looked suspicious, but Barney was definitely relieved.

"Yes," he said. "I can do that! We just go away for a night, and then we come back."

"OK," I said. "Scarborough."

"Scarborough's not even on the list!" Suravi said, like I'd somehow cheated.

"I want to go to York," Maika said.

"Our parents won't have any problem with it," I told them. "We just need somewhere to stay."

"How would we get there?" Barney asked.

"Easy," I said. "Couple of trains, couple of hours." I stared at them all, one by one.

Barney nodded.

Suravi hesitated, looking like she wanted to argue, but she nodded too, reluctantly. "Whatever."

Maika stared back at me.

I opened my mouth, about to tell her she wasn't coming, when she said:

"My mum's friend has a holiday place in Scarborough. We could stay there."

Well, *that* was unexpected. I closed my mouth. She could come, then. I'd just try and avoid her.

The three of them were smiling now. And why not? It was basically just a trip to the seaside. Off on Saturday, back on Sunday. I could feel myself starting to smile too.

Except I was lying to them. Barney, Suravi and Maika would be back on Sunday, but I had a different plan. They'd be going home, but I wouldn't. Because running away suddenly made sense.

I was going to get away from parents and school and cancer. Because now I knew how to do that: I was going to find Uncle Universe.

FOUR

I was in my room, pacing up and down like a prisoner in a cell.

I was thinking about my parents. There they were, making what they thought was my favourite meal and hugging me and crying and, as a result, probably getting indigestion, but they were also sort of saying, "Have you done your homework?" and "Don't forget your football kit!" because actually "Nothing's changed, life is just the same as it's always been!"

In other words, they were treating me like a kid. And the scary thing was, I could definitely see how I might let that happen, how I could just regress, like I was ten years old, and let them tell me what to do. I basically wouldn't have to think. Things would just happen to me.

I didn't want that. That felt wrong. There was no chance in the world that I could **CARRY ON AS NORMAL!**

So I needed to find Uncle Universe. The nickname's a bit childish, but that's because he got it when he was a child. My mum called him Mr Universe when they were growing up, because apparently his brain's as big as the universe. It makes him sound like a superhero, but he's not, he's a real person, my actual uncle, and I could think of four reasons why I wanted to find him:

1. He's brilliant.
2. He's a doctor.
3. Nine years ago, when I was six, he made me a promise.
4. I could live with him for a while. Not for ever, probably, but for a while.

The more I thought about finding him, the more I liked the idea. He'd had a huge argument with my mum years ago, so he'd understand me falling out with my parents. He'd definitely let me stay with him … probably … because of reason three: he'd made a promise.

I used the bathroom, put on my pyjamas and dressing gown, and went downstairs. My parents were watching something boring on TV, and Dad was looking at his phone.

"So, we want to go Scarborough tomorrow," I said. "Me and Barney, Suravi and Maika."

Dad put down his phone, Mum paused the TV. They both looked surprised.

"I thought you and Maika didn't get on these days," Mum said.

They don't know the whole story of what happened in Year 10. If they found out, they'd probably have a huge argument with Maika's mum and talk to the school and God knows what. Which is why I never told them, obviously. Who needs that sort of embarrassment?

"We don't," I said, "but her mum's got a friend with a flat in Scarborough, so it's a sleepover, and it's Barney and Suravi as well."

"And Maika's mum?" Dad said.

I shook my head. "Just the four of us."

Mum raised her eyebrows with a curious smile. "So is there something we should know?" she asked. "You and Suravi? Barney and Maika?"

I stared at her. "What? No! And don't smile at me like that. We're just mates."

"OK," she nodded, hands up in the air. "It was a reasonable question."

"But the thing is," Dad said, "we were wondering if there was anything you'd like to do with us this weekend. Go somewhere, maybe. The cinema, or the football. You could choose whatever you wanted."

"Well," I said, "I want to go to Scarborough."

They looked at each other, and then they looked back at me.

"OK, then," said Mum. She was still nodding and

smiling, but her smile was a bit tight, like she was hiding a much sadder expression behind it. "OK, sweetheart, you should definitely go to Scarborough with your friends, then."

I went back upstairs and paused a minute outside the door to their bedroom, listening to make sure no one was coming up after me. Then I slipped into my parents' room and opened Mum's wardrobe.

There was a whiff of stale air and flowery perfume. And I had a sudden, strange desire to climb right into the wardrobe, pull the door shut after me, wrap my arms around my knees, fold myself into a small ball and just stay there for a while.

I shook my head. *Don't be ridiculous*, I thought to myself. I wasn't going to hide in a wardrobe; I was basically going to do the complete opposite.

There was a pile of stuff at the back of the wardrobe, under the hanging clothes and a couple of folded towels. Years ago, I'd been looking for where my parents had hidden my Christmas presents, and in this dark little corner I'd found old diaries, photograph albums and … yes, address books. I pulled out the most recent one (a green hardback with a picture of a bird on the front) and flicked through the pages. There it was.

HARVEY
SUNNYSIDE COTTAGE,
CLIFF TERRACE,
ROBIN HOOD'S BAY.
YO22 4SC

Harvey was Uncle Universe's real name – Harvey
Knox – but I never called him that; he was always Uncle
Universe. He was my mum's brother, and Robin Hood's
Bay was where he used to live. And hopefully where he *still*
lived. It was a little village on the coast, near Scarborough,
that I'd visited once when I was little. I remembered a
steep hill and small houses, all tightly packed together. I
remembered Uncle Universe and me on the beach, him
holding my wrists, leaning back and spinning me round
and round so that I felt like I was literally flying.

I took a picture of the address with my phone, replaced
the address book, and went back to my room. I pulled
out the shoebox from under my bed, blew dust off the
lid, sneezed, and opened it up. There was an old keyring
with no keys attached, a faded felt-pen picture of a pirate
ship, and there was a letter, addressed to me. Inside the
letter there was a promise. I held it for a moment, rubbed
my thumb over it, smelled it, then I stuffed it into my
rucksack along with a couple of T-shirts and three pairs
of pants.

A text arrived from Barney as I was getting into bed.

So maybe I wasn't as clever as I'd thought. It looked like Barney had sensed there might be more going on than just a weekend in Scarborough. But I couldn't tell him the truth. I didn't want to drag my friends into a search for a man I hadn't seen in about nine years, who might not live at the same address any more, and might not even want to see me if he did. And I definitely couldn't tell them I was planning to stay with him.

I just wanted to get on a train and leave being ill behind, leave my parents behind, leave my friends behind, leave my whole broken life behind.

I replied:

Yep, it's all good!

I lay in bed, wide awake, worrying. I thought about Uncle Universe. When I was little, he used to come and stay over if my parents were working, or when they just needed a break. I remembered board games, ice creams, a visit to Chester Zoo. Then he fell out with my mum, and he never came back. And we never went back to Robin Hood's Bay. I nagged at my parents constantly for a couple of years. *Where is he? When is he*

41

coming to see us? I gave up nagging eventually, but I still missed him.

I yawned and rubbed my aching shoulder. He used to tell me stories. Mum and Dad told me stories too, but they came out of books. Uncle Universe made them up. I asked him once how he did that, and he grinned and told me it was magic. When I was six, I believed him. I thought there was a sort of magical glow around him.

My favourite story was about a boy called Jasper in a village called Oswaldhover, where one day everything in the playground, including Jasper, floated up into the air. It was creepy and strange. I drifted into sleep eventually, and in my dreams I floated off my bed, out of the window and up into the sky, as if I was falling into the stars.

SATURDAY

FIVE

Mum was in the hall. She watched me come downstairs, making me feel self-conscious. Chunky sweater, brown hair hanging neatly to just below her chin, her oval face all crinkly with worry lines around her hazel eyes and her mouth.

She cupped my face in her hands. "You look tired," she said. "It's not too late to change your mind – we can whisk you off pretty much anywhere you want to go. With Barney too, if you like."

I was still annoyed with her, but I felt bad. I decided the best tactic was to change the subject. "When I'm old, do you think I'll get the same lines you've got?" I touched my mouth and my eyes.

She laughed. "Smile more than you frown," she told me, "and you'll only have nice wrinkles when you grow up."

Her lips quivered a bit at those last four words, but she smiled on through. She let go of my face and hugged me tight. I hugged her back.

"OK," I gasped finally, after about ten seconds, "OK, too much hug!"

She let me go and kissed my forehead. "How's your shoulder?"

It was a small, throbby ache pretty much all the time, but I tried not to let it bother me. I put the sensation away in a box and slammed down the lid, because it made me think about Options One, Two and Three and I didn't want to think about them.

"It's a bit achy," I said. I was putting on my shoes. I shrugged both shoulders up and down, revolved them backwards and forwards. "But it's all right."

She nodded. "Love you so much, chickpea," she said.

She hadn't called me "chickpea" for about five years, and it was embarrassing, obviously, but then I said something that I hadn't said for a while too:

"Love you back."

I gave her a last little hug, my arms wrapped round her middle, and then I picked up my bag. I was out of there.

Enough with the soppiness and the awkwardness, the guilt, the hugging and the shoulder shrugging.

I just got going. I was wearing trainers, jeans and my red hoodie. I had a little rucksack on my back and inside it there were two T-shirts, three pairs of underpants, swimming trunks (which I probably wasn't going to use), a sponge bag, some peanut-butter sandwiches, a flapjack, an apple, a bottle of water, and the scrunched-up letter that had been hidden under my bed containing the promise. I also had twenty quid from my parents and all my ready cash in my pocket. A total of thirty-two pounds and seventy-three pence. I had a bank account too, but there was about two pounds fifty in it, so it wasn't much use.

I walked down the snicket, over Keighley Road, up past the garage, and then along the long, boring lane leading to the river, lined by lots of little, boxy houses. Then I took a right up to the frying pan, which is a road that goes up in a straight line and ends in a circular little green surrounded by houses.

Maika's house was three doors along on the left. I don't visit Maika's house any more, because why would I? I used to go to birthday parties there when we were at primary school. There's a rope swing over the river; we used to play on that. More recently, I'd been over sometimes with Suravi and we'd play on the PlayStation. But that was before Maika got mean in Year 10. Really mean. Suddenly, she stopped inviting me round, and if a few mates were meeting in town, she'd just turn round and walk away if I was there. At school, she started making nasty comments all the time, sometimes right to my face and sometimes to my friends behind my back. She'd bump into me and make me drop stuff; she'd trip me up.

I asked Suravi to tell her to stop. She just said, "Maika's having a hard time, you should sit down with her." Even Barney was the same. He was like, "Maybe try talking to her?" I told Suravi I didn't want to sit down with her. "Why doesn't she sit down with me?" I told Barney, "It's gone way beyond talking." And I was right about that, because it just got worse and worse till I ended up in hospital.

So obviously if I'm running away, I'm going to run away with the girl who seems to hate me, right? Because that makes *loads* of sense.

But here I was, outside her door. I knocked, hoping I wouldn't be the first to arrive. Maika's mum opened up. Great big smile, stripy T-shirt, towel on her head. I'd always liked Maika's mum.

"Jasper! You're the first to arrive. I feel like I haven't seen you for about a hundred years. Come here."

She grabbed me and pulled me in for a hug and I was squashed up against her, but I didn't mind that because she'd always been so nice to me. She stepped away eventually, but she kept her hands on my shoulders. It was a morning for mums grabbing me, apparently.

"I'm so sorry this has happened to you, Jasper." Her eyes were big and honest, and they found mine and somehow held on to them so I couldn't look away. "But they're going to fix you right up, you hear? Don't you worry about that. Now come on in, you're the first. Did I say that already?"

Maika's mum was clever. She managed to say she was sorry without it being awkward or embarrassing. I'm not sure how she did that. I followed her into the kitchen and Maika was at the table, sitting there looking a bit nervous. Probably because we'd never actually talked about everything that happened last year, and now here I was in her house.

"Look who it is, darling." Maika's mum sort of showed me to Maika, like she might not have noticed me. Then she turned to me again. "Why's it so long since you've been round at ours?"

"Oh, yes," I said, smiling vaguely, "I don't know."

"Maika, get the kettle on, and get the biscuits. I've got to finish my hair."

And then she was gone, and it was just me and Maika in the kitchen together.

Awkward.

I couldn't remember the last time I'd been alone in a room with her. I stood there ... and she sat there ... and neither of us said anything. *Very awkward.* The truth was I missed her. She'd been one of my best friends, but now there was this barrier between us.

She was biting her lower lip. I was biting the inside of my cheek. There was a lot of biting going on. It was so awkward that it probably would have lightened things up if she'd told me she was sorry I had cancer ... again.

"Want tea?" she said. "Coffee?" It was pretty

impressive – even when she was offering me a drink, she managed to sound irritated.

"Thanks."

She got up, put the kettle on and got out a tin of those rectangular biscuits with the thick chocolate on.

"Love these," I said.

And then neither of us said anything else for about seven seconds. Me crunching the biscuit was the only noise, and it seemed like it was in Dolby surround sound. But then suddenly we both spoke.

"OK," she began, her voice slow and careful. "I want to tell you…"

But I started talking at the same moment, only not so much talking as blurting, my voice quick and loud, as if we were in the middle of an argument: "Why did you, all that time, suddenly you were horrible, what was that about?"

I didn't even know where those words came from, I definitely hadn't planned them – it was like they just erupted out of my mouth without warning. I guess that means they must have been stored inside my head for a long time.

Maika went red, her mouth went small and tight and I wasn't sure if she was about to shout at me or cry, but then there was a knock on the front door and she ran out of the kitchen.

So … things were off to a great start. *Brilliant*. The kettle gurgled then snapped off, and I made myself an instant coffee. "*I want to tell you…*" Tell me what? I was annoyed with myself for blurting, but also it was fair enough, wasn't it? I had reason to blurt, didn't I? I was having this whole serious and pretty intense discussion with myself in my head when Maika came back with Barney and Suravi. Barney was leading his little dog, Milo, which looks like a mop with a face.

"You've brought Milo," I said.

He looked genuinely surprised by my surprise. "Of course I've brought Milo! He'd be lonely if I went away without him."

Barney likes animals, and he loves his little dog. I should have guessed he'd bring him. And to be fair, he is a really nice dog. He's rusty red with a bright green collar and pointy ears, and his little pink tongue is always hanging out. He'll sort of point his nose at you and lift his head, like he's thinking about asking you a question.

I was probably lucky Barney hadn't brought his iguana too.

"I've got Milo, my harmonica, my book and my lunch," he said, patting his bag. "All the essentials."

Barney loves his harmonica almost as much as he loves Milo. He's always in the music room at school, practising.

"Right," I said. "OK, so we're running away with a dog." I looked at Suravi. "Have you brought Chunky?"

Hamsters are only supposed to live for two or three years, and Suravi's had hers since she was twelve. We always joke that she's been replaced, like, five times already by her parents. She smiled and opened her bag. "Funny you should say that…"

"No!" I said. "No way! You haven't brought her?"

She lifted up her hands. "Of course I haven't! I was joking, you muppet!" she squealed.

"You sound like Chunky," I told her.

"You look like Chunky," she told me.

Barney had found the biscuits, and he had two in his mouth. "We going then?" he asked, even though it was almost impossible to understand him through the biscuits. "Or not?" Crumbs sprayed out of his mouth on to the floor.

Milo barked. He was either enthusiastic about leaving, or he just wanted a biscuit.

Maika's mum came back in, towel no longer on her head.

"Everything all right, lovelies?" she asked, her forehead creased and her eyes a bit squinty. She looked at each of us. "Are you definitely up for this?"

Maika, Suravi and Barney looked at me. So Maika's mum looked at me too. I felt like my skin had just got a bit tighter than usual. My hand went to my shoulder and I rubbed it gently. A couple of seconds passed with everyone staring at me.

I thought about my plan: the others leaving on Sunday, me alone in Scarborough, getting a cab or a bus to Robin

Hood's Bay, not even knowing if Uncle Universe would be there.

I swallowed nervously. "Yes," I said. "Of course."

The others agreed.

"OK," I said with a tense smile. "Let's go, then!"

Maika's mum held up her index finger. "Hold your actual horses," she said. "Some things I need to clarify." She took a slow breath. We waited for her to speak. She wasn't a teacher, she owned a café in town, but she acted like a teacher now, waiting for the class to settle down so that she could be sure everyone was listening.

"Right," she said. "Let's just get this straight. The four of you are going to my friend's flat, which will be empty. Maika's got the keys, and I've given her money to order a takeaway tonight. I've been in touch with your beloved parents and we all agree, we'd like you back in your respective homes by six p.m. tomorrow. OK?" She looked at each of us, and we all nodded at her seriously. "OK!" And suddenly she was smiling again. "Well, have a lovely time, then. Build a sandcastle, have an ice cream at the Harbour Bar, go on a boat trip round the bay, and I'll see you tomorrow."

We shuffled out of the door, getting in each other's way. She stood there and smiled and waved and smiled and waved, and then, finally, she was out of sight.

We were on our way to Scarborough.

SIX

"You sure you know where your mum's friend's flat is?" Barney asked.

We were on the towpath, heading towards the station. Geese honked at us and splashed into the canal as we approached. Milo barked at them.

"What if we can't find it?" Barney continued. He was obviously nervous. His voice went quiet, as if he was talking to himself. "What if you lose the key?"

"I won't!" Maika sounded as though she'd already run out of patience, and we'd only left her house like five minutes ago.

Suravi was walking next to me. "You and Maika," she whispered, "you need to sort out your issues on this trip."

I stared at her. "What are you talking about? How is any of this on me?"

She shook her head. "Sort it out."

And then she sped up and walked next to Maika, before I could say anything else. I stared at her and Maika's backs. So, what, I should just forget how I ended up in hospital? We were back to *You should sit down with her, talk to her.* And it still didn't seem fair to me at all. She was the bad guy here; it was up to her to make it right. If that was even possible.

We were a funny sort of group. I hadn't thought we'd all be singing songs together and swearing to be best friends for ever, but I'd thought we might at least get along with each other. The problem was, we all liked at least one other person in the group but none of us liked everyone. Barney didn't like Maika because of my history with her, and Suravi seemed pretty indifferent about Barney. You could see it in how we walked along the towpath: Suravi and Maika next to each other in front; me, Barney and Milo behind; Suravi looking back over her shoulder talking to me; Maika staring straight ahead; Barney looking at a goose.

"What we've got to do," Suravi was saying to me, head twisted over her shoulder, "is find Perfect Moments."

(You could hear the capital letters in the way she said it.)

I stared at her. "What?"

"I read it in my mum's *Cosmopolitan*."

"I saw it first," Maika said, still staring straight ahead.

"Maika saw it first," Suravi agreed. "You search for Perfect Moments and you try and have at least one every

55

day, because it makes you …" – she trailed off and looked at Maika – "what was the word?"

"Replenished," said Maika.

"What's that supposed to mean?" asked Barney.

"Recharged," said Suravi. "Like when you charge your phone. So that's what we have to do today and tomorrow. Find Perfect Moments to recharge ourselves."

"OK," I said. I had no idea what she was on about, but it sounded like she was saying this weekend was about making me feel better about having cancer. Which was actually annoying – this wasn't meant to be some woo-woo, inspirational slogan kind of trip. "Replenish your soul!" What I wanted – until I went looking for Uncle Universe – was to *not* think about being ill. But I didn't say anything, because it's usually easiest to agree with Suravi.

She stopped twisting her head over her shoulder, which was just as well because I'd been worried she was going to fall into the canal. Barney looked at me and shrugged. I looked at him and rolled my eyes. *Perfect Moments.* As if.

Our parents had booked our tickets in advance, so we got them out of the machine and jumped on to the York train. We found a table, we all got our phones out, and Barney retrieved his book and his sandwiches from his backpack. He started eating. He fed a bit of bread to Milo, who was sitting at his feet, thwacking his tail on the floor.

After a minute or two, he looked up from his book,

swallowed his mouthful and smiled at Suravi. "I like your T-shirt," he said.

"What?" She frowned at him, not sure if he was taking the piss. It was just a plain blue T-shirt.

He blushed, took another bite of his sandwich and looked back down at his book.

After that no one spoke for a while. I wanted to say something to cheer up Barney because he was embarrassed and actually looked pretty gloomy, but I couldn't think of anything. I sensed there was an air of "What are we doing here?" to be honest, because we all just sat there and none of us seemed to know what to say. I was wishing Maika wasn't there, because that would probably have improved the atmosphere, but I also knew that was unfair, since it was her mum's friend's flat that was making this whole trip possible. It was frustrating because I felt like I should be in a good mood. The trip was the perfect way to get close to Robin Hood's Bay, and it was also a chance to spend the weekend at the seaside with my two best friends. And Maika.

I looked at her out of the corner of my eye as she stared out of the window. She had her hand over her mouth and her eyes were thoughtful, like she was working out the answer to some big question. She had a small, brown mole near her left ear. Her fingers tapped her lips and she smiled a little as we passed a bit of scrubby ground with some horses in it.

I remembered walking across a field with Maika a couple of years ago, on the way to a friend's house. A horse had cantered over to us and bared its scary, alien teeth, and then butted her. We ran away and it ran alongside us, so we tumbled over a dry-stone wall to escape. I smiled at the memory, the two of us side by side on the grass, leaning on the wall, leaning on each other, shocked and laughing.

Then Maika turned and caught me looking at her.

"What?" she said. Her face went from smiling and thoughtful to hard and suspicious in about half a second.

"Nothing," I said. I nodded at the window. "Horses."

Maybe Suravi was right, maybe somehow, sometime this weekend, I could forgive her, if she properly apologized for everything. I thought I'd like that, but it didn't seem likely.

I looked at Suravi. "So," I said, "what really happened yesterday, with the whole chair thing? You told them you were provoked, right?"

"Don't want to talk about it," she said.

To be fair, it wasn't just Maika making the atmosphere a bit tense.

I checked my phone. Text from Mum already.

Everything OK? xx

I replied:

58

But everything wasn't OK. Not really.

I stared out of the window thinking about tomorrow, when Barney, Suravi and Maika would all be getting back on the train and I'd be going my separate way, alone.

I wasn't even certain that Uncle Universe would be happy about me turning up at his front door, even though I had the letter which contained the promise. He'd had that huge argument with my mum all those years ago, so perhaps he wouldn't want to see me, let alone let me stay with him. Then what would I do?

It wasn't a *completely* ridiculous plan, but it certainly wasn't totally rational either.

"What you thinking?"

This was Barney, looking up from his book. He'd already finished his lunchtime sandwiches, even though it was only five past ten.

"Nothing," I said.

He gave me a look that said he didn't believe me, but I ignored him.

"What're we going to do in Scarborough?" I asked.

So we talked about ice cream, and whether we were going to swim, and Barney wanted to know what takeaway we were going to get. At Bradford the train entered the station forwards and left it backwards, which is alarming if you're not expecting it, because you think

59

at first you're heading home again but you're not, you're still on the way to Leeds.

Suravi looked up and down the aisle, then opened her puffy green coat and took something out of an inside pocket.

"I brought this," she said.

It was a metal star. "What is it?" I asked. "A brooch?" She was sort of hiding it behind her coat so no stranger could see it. Maybe it was valuable, a family heirloom? Or did she steal it?

She puffed out a laugh. "No, you fool, it's not a brooch, it's a ninja throwing star."

Barney was staring at her. "Why did you bring that?" he asked.

She nodded wisely. "Just in case."

"In case of what?" I asked. "Ninjas?"

We got to Leeds, and I looked through the window at the train across the platform. An announcement said it was going to York.

"Let's get on that one," I said.

"No," Barney said.

"It'll be a fast train, faster than this one."

"I'm not moving!" Barney insisted. "We'll get out, we'll miss the train, we'll get split up – it'll all go horribly wrong."

Barney's always worried about things going horribly wrong. He told me at the beginning of this school year

60

that he was working on it, that he was going to be braver. I haven't noticed any difference, other than his haircut. He got his hair shaved at the sides to make himself look tougher. Didn't work. He gets called "moon face" at school by kids like Joe Hancock.

"All right, disaster boy," Suravi said. "Calm down. We'll stay on this one."

I was right, though, the other train would have been faster. Our train was like a bus, chugging slowly out of Leeds and stopping at loads of places, slowing down slowly, speeding up slowly. We went through East Somewhere and Church Something and a lot of fields; we saw some of those shaggy red cows with the big horns, and then at last we reached York.

Suravi had her phone out, checking timetables.

"Scarborough train in four minutes," she said. "Shall we go for it?"

"Yes!" I said. "Let's go!"

"No," Maika said, frowning at me. "What's the rush? And who put you in charge anyway?"

I mean, this whole trip was all about me. But she didn't look like she'd react well to me saying so.

"I agree with Maika," Barney said, which was annoying of him, but I knew he was still worried about getting split up.

So I didn't say anything. We got out in no big hurry and checked when the next train to Scarborough was.

Twenty minutes, not too bad. We found a café, then Maika went to the loo.

"Can we even afford drinks and buns?" Barney asked. "Cos I'm hungry." And then he bought a can of Coke and a blueberry muffin without waiting for an answer. "Does this count as a Perfect Moment?" he asked, with his mouth all puffed out like Suravi's hamster. "Because it's a nice muffin."

"No," Suravi said. "It doesn't."

We decided we'd check how much cash we all had when Maika came back. Suravi thought we should pool it and decide together what we wanted to spend it on. I didn't like that idea, because my money had to last past Sunday, although I couldn't tell her that because it was a whole big secret.

We couldn't get into that argument, though, because Maika didn't come back.

"I'll check on her," Suravi eventually said.

We all went to the ladies' loos and Suravi went inside. She came out again almost immediately, looking worried.

"She's not there."

"What? Where is she, then?" I asked.

Suravi was looking around the station. Barney croaked out a sound like someone had a hand on his throat.

"Oh my God," he gasped. "Maika's been kidnapped!"

SEVEN

"Maika! Where are you?"

Suravi was shouting into her phone, leaving a message, spinning on the spot, looking everywhere. Barney and I were back-to-back, looking all around the station, trying to catch sight of her. Blonde hair, taller than Barney. She'd been wearing a pink denim jacket with white panels in it. She shouldn't have been hard to spot, but there was no sign of her.

"Should we tell the police?" Barney asked, jabbing a finger at two uniformed officers standing under the departures board.

"No!" I said quickly. I didn't want my whole plan to end before lunchtime on the first day. *It couldn't end this quickly, could it?* I sort of danced on my toes for a moment. "OK, yes!" I said, because I realized that of course my plan wasn't the most important thing any more, because Maika had literally disappeared.

Barney and I sprinted towards the two police officers, a man and a woman in bulky bright-yellow jackets. The man spotted us approaching.

"Wait!"

Suravi was shouting at us, waving, staring at her phone.

We paused, caught between Suravi behind us and the police officers in front. The policeman came towards us. "All right, lads?" he asked.

Suravi ran over. "My mum's meeting us, thought we'd lost her, but we didn't," she gabbled breathlessly, pointing vaguely at the platforms. "So we're fine, thanks, we're fine."

The policeman looked around theatrically. "OK. Glad you found her." He nodded. "Where is she, then?"

"Outside," Suravi said. "With the car. Thanks, bye!"

He scrunched his eyes, puzzled. Suravi was definitely overdoing it. "Hold on a minute," he said. "You all seem a bit tense. Want to tell me what's up?"

"No," I said. It came out sharper than I intended.

He raised his eyebrows. "No?"

"Nothing's up!" I said. "We're going to find" – I pointed at Suravi – "her mum."

He nodded. "OK. I'll come with you."

"No need," said Suravi. "Gotta go!"

And suddenly she was running off. I looked at the policeman, shrugged, and ran after her, Barney beside me with Milo. When I looked over my shoulder the policeman was still standing there, watching us, holding the lapels of his shiny jacket.

My little rucksack was bumping on my back, rubbing the aching lump on my shoulder, Milo was barking like this was all a great game, Barney was panting next to me, and Suravi was well ahead. I always used to win every race on Sports Day – well, either I did or Maika did – but Suravi had had a good start, and I'd had an actual operation with a general anaesthetic and everything not long ago. OK, it was a small operation and it was on my shoulder, not my leg, but still.

We sprinted out of the station and turned left, out from under the canopy to a twisty bit of road where cars could come in and out.

And there was Maika. Just sitting on the low wall, waiting for us.

"You disappeared!" I panted.

"What's going on?" Suravi asked.

"We thought you'd been kidnapped!" Barney gasped.

Milo barked.

Maika just stared at us. Her face was doing a complicated, squashed thing, where she looked cross but also embarrassed. A van went round the twisty bit of road behind her. It stank of exhaust, and when it braked it made a noise like cutlery being dropped on the floor. She waited till it had gone past.

"I told you I wanted to go to York," she said, "and

look" – she waved a hand around her – "we're in York, aren't we? I don't want to shoot off when we only just got here."

She pushed her lips out. Her face went from cross and embarrassed to stubborn and upset. I opened my mouth to speak, but Suravi lifted her finger high in the air to stop me. She sat on the wall next to Maika and gave us a look, which clearly said, *Back off*.

"What's up?" she said, like the policeman, only not really like the policeman at all.

Barney and I moved away while the girls talked. I told Barney I couldn't believe it. Somehow Maika was making this trip all about her. Barney agreed, and Milo ran round us, twisting his lead around our legs, which wasn't helpful at all. Suravi and Maika totally ignored us, heads close together, shoulders hunched, hands moving, looking all intense and important.

"Right," Suravi said eventually, standing up. "We're having a little detour."

"What?" I said. "No, we need to go to Scarborough. That's the plan."

She held up her finger again. "No, see, this is part of the problem: you being bossy."

So on the one hand, Suravi is always right … usually … but on the other hand, this wasn't making any sense. This whole trip was my thing, but now Maika and Suravi seemed to be hijacking it. I was going to answer her – I was going to say, *This whole trip is my thing!* but I saw someone over her shoulder before I had the chance. It was the policeman from inside the station, and he was striding towards us.

Suravi pointed. "That's our bus, come on!"

Suddenly, she and Maika were running across the road for a number sixty-six bus, Barney and me following. "And *I'm* the bossy one?" I panted.

He was panting too. "Well," he said, "sometimes."

I hadn't expected him to say that, but there wasn't time to talk about it.

The policeman shouted at us, "Hey, wait!" But we didn't wait, we jumped on the bus. The copper stood there and watched the bus pulling away. He was frowning.

"All right," I said, as we fell on to the seat at the back and looked out of the window, "now we're on the run from the Law."

Suravi laughed. "Well, I reckon we got away."

"But why are we even here?" I asked.

"OK," said Suravi, her voice all cool and soothing. "First of all, calm down—"

"Can't she speak for herself?" I interrupted, pointing a finger across her at Maika.

Maika turned bright red. Her nostrils flared and her eyes squinched.

"I want to see my sister," she hissed. "Is that all right with you?"

I swallowed. *I mean, no, it wasn't all right with me, not really, because hello, we're meant to be going to Scarborough?* But I didn't say that.

"I don't want to be *bossy*," I told her, trying to keep my voice all calm and reasonable, "but I thought this was, basically, mostly, about me. Isn't it?"

Suravi sort of patted the air. "Detour," she said. "Like I told you two minutes ago. You've got to listen, Jasper. It's just a small detour, and then we'll get back on track. Literally."

I leant my head on the window and stared out, trying to squash down my temper. We were going to see Maika's sister. *What the hell? Who's next, Barney's second cousins in Whitby?*

I watched red-bricked terraced houses pass by.

Isn't York meant to be really old? Like, Roman? Or Viking? I was pretty sure those houses weren't Roman.

This didn't feel right at all.

Andi was waiting at the bus stop. She was leaning on a wall with her hands in the pockets of her suede jacket. She looked up as the bus arrived, her eyes scanning the windows. I hadn't seen her for a couple of years, and I had to try not to stare. She had the same slim face as Maika, but her blonde hair was longer and tousled. She had a bit of a tan and freckles, and when she saw her sister a smile stretched across her face, and seriously, she looked like pretty much the coolest person I'd ever seen. As we all got out, she put an arm round Maika, ignoring the rest of us at first. "You OK?" I heard her say to her sister. "You sure?" Seemed a bit dramatic, to be honest.

We went on to the York University campus and sat by the lake, with geese strutting around, giving us evil looks with their small black eyes. Andi bought us Cokes, which I had to admit was nice of her, and Barney bought himself another sandwich. Me, Suravi and Maika got out our packed lunches.

Andi looked at us and shook her head. She was relaxed now she'd had that quick little check-in with her sister. "Guys," she said, "this isn't what running away looks like. This is literally a picnic."

"You told her?" Barney said, glaring at Maika. He looked at Andi. "It's not really running away. It's just for the weekend."

Andi's eyes flicked between us, settling on me. She looked curious, but I was still cross, so I turned away, frowning. And that's when I saw something surprising in Maika's green rucksack.

As she took her lunch out, she half pulled out a doll along with it. A blonde Barbie doll in a frilly, flowery dress. She shoved it back in quickly, but she caught me looking and glared at me. It was quite tempting to make a sarky comment about her carrying around a secret Barbie, but I didn't need the stress that would probably cause.

Barney, I noticed, didn't have his book out. He was just gazing at Andi, who had taken off her suede jacket and was scratching Milo behind his ears. He definitely wasn't looking gloomy any more. Maybe he'd decided he preferred Andi to Suravi. She leant back on her elbows, closed her eyes and tipped her freckly face towards the warm sun.

Being at university seemed like a nice thing. The grass smelled grassy, a goose splashed into the lake, and I took a bite of the homemade flapjack Mum had packed for me. All right, the police might be looking for us, but they weren't going to find us here.

Maybe being in York wasn't that bad after all.

I glanced at Suravi. "Is this a Perfect Moment?" I asked.

She shook her head, showing me her sandwich. "Cheese," she said, "the most boring sandwich in the world. Definitely not perfect."

Barney was still gazing at Andi. "What are you studying?" he asked her.

"Physics with astrophysics," Andi told him.

"What's that actually mean?" he persisted.

"It means a lot," she smiled. "Pretty much everything. Including the stuff we don't understand. So, for instance, dark energy makes up most of the universe, and no one really knows what it is. Other than dark. Which is interesting." She looked at Barney. "What subject do you like best?"

Barney's voice was more enthusiastic than normal. "English, because I love reading. But geography too, cos we might go to Iceland. The country, not the supermarket."

Andi nodded. "Sounds good."

She looked at me. Her smile was sympathetic and calm, her green-blue eyes were curious, and my last bit of crossness melted away. *Seriously, how could Maika have a sister as nice as this?*

"So, why Scarborough?"

I didn't want to lie to her. Her gentle smiling face made me want to tell the truth. But I did lie to her.

"Because we all like the beach," I said, shrugging.

"I wanted us to go to Edinburgh and get jobs but Jasper vetoed that idea," Suravi told her.

Andi smiled and nodded, but she was still staring at me. "It's not just the beach, though, is it?" she said. "You're sitting there all quiet, and I'm wondering what's going on in your head."

She was annoyingly perceptive. Maybe she could see dark energy floating around me. I looked back at her, trying to meet her eyes.

"I wanted to get away from everything at home that was getting me down," I said. "Including being ill."

"Well, that's fair enough." She nodded slowly, still looking at me. "But you'll be home again tomorrow?"

I nodded right back at her. "Tomorrow."

So it was partly the truth and partly not. I didn't feel good about lying to her, but I was already lying to everyone else, so it didn't make much difference. I'd lie, I'd watch my friends go back home without me, and I'd do just about anything to complete the plan, to find Uncle Universe, and run away properly.

EIGHT

Maika and Andi hugged at the bus stop.

I don't usually mind not having a sibling, but when I saw Maika put her arms round her big sister and hold her close, I thought perhaps I did. Barney and Suravi both have younger brothers and mostly they seem to find them irritating but there was something about that warm, soppy hug that looked good to me.

"Take care, honey," Andi told Maika. Then she looked at us. "You too," she said.

We all nodded, although I wasn't sure what taking care would look like in my situation. It would probably mean going home, and I wasn't going to do that.

We got on our bus.

Maika stared out of the window, clearly not wanting to talk to anyone. Suravi looked preoccupied. Barney had Milo on his lap and was rubbing noses with him. He didn't seem quite so gloomy any more, but he wasn't exactly smiling either. Maybe it hadn't been a Perfect Moment, but seeing Andi had injected some positive energy into our day, and that feeling had drained away the minute we stepped back on the bus. I felt bad, as if I'd invited them all round to mine and they weren't having a good time. These were my two best friends, plus someone who used to be my best friend, and I wanted them to be glad that they were doing this thing with me.

I checked the time. "Well," I said, "I don't want to be *bossy*, but maybe we shouldn't shoot off when we've only just got here?"

I was deliberately repeating what Maika had said outside the station. She turned away from the window, curious. Suravi looked at me. She'd been miles away, and I saw her slowly digesting what I'd just said. And then she smiled.

We jumped off the bus at the top of Piccadilly and walked into a wide pedestrianized street. I bought hot waffles covered in chocolate sauce at a stall and handed them out, while Suravi bought an ice cream. "We'll run out of money!" Barney protested. Maika replied quietly, like she expected to be shouted down, "We could always busk?"

We all stared at her. She had a waffle in her hand and chocolate sauce on her chin. She was raising her eyebrows and smiling like it was a sensible idea and not completely out of the question.

"I'm lead singer," she said. She pointed her finger at each of us. "Barney on his harmonica, you two backing vocals."

I shook my head. I wanted everyone to have a good time, but there were limits. "No," I said. "No, no, no. I can't sing! Not going to happen."

Barney suggested some tunes he'd learned from YouTube tutorials.

Maika laughed. "My mum's favourites," she said. She found the lyrics on her phone, and then suddenly there we were, outside Marks & Spencer with Milo's food bowl in front of us.

Barney played "Blowin' in the Wind" by Bob Dylan, and then "Imagine" and "Hey Jude". He had his eyes closed the whole time. He made a few mistakes, but he actually sounded pretty good. In fact, he looked quite cool, not like a teddy bear at all.

Maika was amazing. At first, she was tentative, but as she got more confident, her voice got louder. It had a bright, simple clarity and proper emotion vibrating inside the words. Suravi threw herself into singing along, but wasn't completely in tune, and I droned along nervously, looking mostly at the ground, doing my best.

People stopped and watched. Maika really was brilliant. I'd only ever heard her in a choir before, and that was years ago. This was a whole new side to her. Suddenly she was the centre of attention and showing off a serious talent. It's funny how you think you know someone quite well, and it turns out you don't know them at all.

We'd made four pounds and seventy-two pence when a beardy bloke with a leather jacket, a guitar and an amplifier showed up. His eyes flicked over all four of us. He looked serious. "This is my pitch, guys," he said.

"OK," I said quickly. "Sorry, we'll go!"

I was about to pick up our money but Suravi, of course, wasn't moving.

"*Your* pitch?" she snapped. "Who says?"

The guy stared at her. He had a small, black beard and he was enormous – he looked like he could literally pick us all up and chuck us into Marks & Spencer. He stared for a couple of seconds, and then he laughed. "The council says," he told her. "I've got a licence."

There wasn't much we could say to that.

He turned to Maika and Barney. "You're pretty good, by the way," he told them. "Wanna do a song together before you go?"

And that was how we ended up playing "Hallelujah" with Noah – that was his name – on guitar, crooning soulfully in harmony with Maika, while Barney did his eyes closed, haunting harmonica thing. Maika really went for it. There was a lovely sweetness and a heartbreaking sadness in her voice, and when she climbed up towards the top notes you felt like you climbed with her, all the way up, so suddenly you were holding your breath, full of hope.

I watched her, hands behind her back, chin raised, singing like that. I felt a deep ache in my chest and a wave of sadness. It wasn't just the song, it was her, Maika; it was knowing that somewhere along the way, I'd lost my friend.

I focused on my own terrible singing to take my mind off my feelings. I told myself it was probably the melancholy song that was making me sad anyway, not Maika.

We got an actual crowd around us, and when we'd finished, they applauded. I mean, they *really* applauded – someone even whooped. Milo's bowl got a whole load of coins in it.

Noah nodded at Maika and Barney. "You've got skills, guys," he told them.

Barney blushed, and Maika looked delighted. We split the money in the bowl, which meant we got another ten pounds to go with our four seventy-two, then we thanked Noah, Barney high-fived him, and we left him to it.

"Wow," said Barney, as we walked away, "we should totally form a band."

"You three should," I said.

"Yeah." Suravi smiled, pointing at me. "*You* were rubbish!"

"But you were brilliant," Barney told Suravi, totally earnestly.

Suravi rolled her eyes, and Maika smiled.

"We need a name. How about The Iguanas?" said Barney. He looked at Suravi. "What d'you think?"

"I'm not going to be in a band called The Iguanas!" Maika protested, before Suravi could speak.

We walked back to the station, laughing and chatting the whole way, as if I didn't have cancer and life really was normal. I even spotted a bit of Roman wall, but Suravi said nobody cared.

Then, as we approached the station, the mood changed.

"What if that policeman's still there?" Barney asked.

Suravi shrugged. "We haven't done anything wrong."

"Except you lied to him," Barney told her. "And Jasper said he didn't want to tell him what was going on, and then we ran off when he came out, and he said 'Wait' and we didn't wait."

Suravi laughed. "OK, but apart from all that, we're golden."

"We might get arrested," Barney said, "and never get to Scarborough."

Suravi shrugged again, which wasn't a great argument.

We stood there, nobody moving, just staring warily at the station up ahead, as if it was a really tricky level in a video game.

NINE

"I've got an idea," Maika said eventually. "If they're looking for us, they're looking for two boys and two girls." She looked at me and Barney. "So one of you two should pretend to be a girl."

Suravi cackled. Barney and I just stared at Maika.

"Three girls and a boy," Maika said. "Not what they're looking for."

"OK," I said, "One: no. No way. Two: neither of us look like girls. And three: no, absolutely no way."

Maika pointed a finger right at my nose. "Long hair, eyelashes, pouty lips. Are you sure you aren't actually a girl?"

"I've got eyelashes," Barney said.

We all ignored him. I stared at Maika, not sure if she was insulting me or complimenting me. I frowned at her, just to be safe. "Right," I said. "Even if they're still there, they're probably not looking for us, but we can split up, just in case. We'll meet on the train and no one will even notice us."

"I don't want to split up!" Barney said immediately. "That's what they do in horror films, and then everyone dies."

"This isn't a horror film," Suravi told him. "There's not an axe murderer in a clown mask running around after lunch in York station."

"What's wrong with looking like a girl, anyway?" Maika asked me. "Are you a misogynist?"

"No!" I said. "Of course not!" My voice was an actual squeak now. I lowered it. "I'd do it if I thought it would work, but it definitely *won't* work, which is why I won't do it!"

I checked my phone.

"There's a train about to leave," I said. "Let's just go straight to the platform and jump right on it." I clapped my hands. "We'll be fine, everything will be fine!"

We stepped cautiously through the main door of the station. There was a wide hallway containing stalls selling cards and cakes. No police.

"See?" I said, relieved. "They're long gone."

We hurried down a passage past a café to the platforms, and there they were, the same two police officers, standing under the departures board again. We ducked and ran in the opposite direction, past Smiths and up the stairs to the other platforms.

"Did they see us?" I hissed.

"Don't know," Suravi said. "Just move."

We sprinted across the bridge: me and Maika in front – just like we always were on Sports Day in primary school – and Suravi, Barney and Milo right behind. As I headed down the steps to our platform, I looked over my shoulder.

Oh no.

"Hey!" the policeman shouted. "Wait!"

Why was he obsessed with us? Did we really look so suspicious?

"Quick!" I said.

We ran down the steps and jumped on our train as the doors were closing, panting, laughing nervously as we found seats.

"Oh my God!" Maika exclaimed.

"That was so close!" Suravi said.

The policeman was standing on the platform, watching the train leave, talking into his radio. Which was slightly worrying.

Milo barked.

"I can't believe we did that!" Barney gasped. "We are officially fugitives – on the run from justice!"

A familiar silence settled over us. But this time there was no awkward sense of *What are we doing here?* It felt more like *OK, I need a breather now.* We didn't even get our phones out; we just sat there and took a moment. Today had been a lot: we'd had Maika disappearing, the police chasing us, Andi and busking, and then the police chasing us *again*. We needed a bit of a rest, thanks very much.

I leant my head against the window. It vibrated against my forehead and it wasn't very comfortable, but I kept it there as I looked out across the countryside. There was a field with shallow holes in it, each filled by a sheep sheltering from the wind. Then a pond with someone sitting on a small jetty, fishing. I wanted to be him. Sitting there in September sunshine, wearing a warm coat, ready for a bite but in no particular hurry. Perhaps there'd be no bite, my fishing rod wouldn't bend, but I'd just sit there anyway while trains passed behind me and sheep stood in holes and the sun shone. That would be all right. No police after me, no guilt about lying to my parents. No Option Three.

Maybe I could get all that at Robin Hood's Bay with Uncle Universe.

I was trying to be optimistic, but it was difficult. Because it was still there, behind everything else. Option Three. It was always still there – the ugly black toad living inside my skull – and whenever it was quiet, when nothing else was going on, it sort of shifted around and croaked. I rubbed my achy shoulder. *Does it ache more now than it did a week ago? If so, does that mean it's started spreading?*

"Hey," said Suravi.

I looked at her.

"You all right?"

I forced a smile. "Of course."

She narrowed her eyes a bit, but she didn't argue with me. "Want to talk?"

"No," I said. "Thanks."

The phrase *It's gone way beyond talking* slipped into my head and I glanced at Maika. She was looking at me, and our eyes met briefly then darted away again. I sighed.

We were stopping at Malton. We'd be at Scarborough in half an hour.

"That policeman might have radioed for someone to watch out for us," I said. "So we should look different, we should at least change our tops. And forget horror movies: we definitely need to split up when we get off."

Suravi coughed, and as she coughed, she said, "Bossy."

I tutted, but Maika shook her head. "He's right," she said.

Well, that was surprising, but also ... pleasing. I took off my red hoodie, Suravi, Maika and Barney took their coats off, and we stuffed them in our bags. Maika got a grey hoodie out and pulled it on. She pulled up the hood and looked at me.

"See, it's not difficult," she said. "I'm a boy."

I looked at her. Her serious eyes, bluey-green like her sister's, her cheekbones, her pursed lips. The mole by her left ear. She didn't look like a boy to me. I realized I was staring, so I looked away.

The ticket inspector came down the aisle.

She looked at the four of us and smiled. "Little holiday, is it?" she said.

"We're meeting my mum in Scarborough," Suravi told her, smiling back. She can turn on a big, bright, friendly smile when she wants to. "Me and the boys."

"Alrighty then," the inspector said. "Have a great time."

"Thank you," I said. We were liars, but we were polite, smiley liars.

The train slowed down, rumbling, brakes sighing, and we pulled into Scarborough at last. We split up, each of us leaving by different doors. ("No one's going to die," I told Barney.)

I walked close to a couple arguing about taxis so it looked like I was with them.

Maika was in front of me, hands in the pockets of her hoodie, kicking a stone. I supposed she could have been mistaken for a boy, from behind.

Barney was ahead of her, looking exactly like he always did. His walk was hesitant, short steps then longer ones, a little skip to the left or right as if he didn't know where he was going. That was fair enough here in Scarborough, but he'd walk like that down a corridor in school too. He looked over his shoulder and caught my eye, which he wasn't supposed to do.

Suravi was behind me. I glanced back. She'd actually started a conversation with a young couple, and she was

84

swaggering along like she was with a bunch of admiring friends.

There was a ticket collector by the barriers, watching people going through. His eyes were narrowed and wrinkles ran along his forehead as if he was trying to read tiny letters on a page. Had he been asked to look out for four unaccompanied teenagers, travelling together? A puffy green coat, red hoodie, pink denim? I took a deep breath and told myself he'd be watching people through the barriers anyway.

"Nice and sunny, isn't it?" I said to the woman in front of me, who'd just finished arguing about taxis. She looked a bit surprised, then glanced up at the cloudy sky and shrugged. I nodded, like we were having an interesting chat. "Yeah, cos it was really cold last week." She smiled uncertainly and looked away, but hopefully it looked like we were together.

We all got through. Either the man wasn't looking at all, or he wasn't looking very carefully.

And that was it.

We'd arrived.

I was standing outside the station in actual Scarborough. I'd taken a huge step away from home and a huge step towards finding Uncle Universe. I was doing it. I was properly running away from everything.

TEN

"Race you to the beach!" Suravi yelled.

We'd crossed the road from the station and were on what felt like a High Street, and suddenly Suravi was running away from us. We all dashed after her, like Olympic sprinters, Milo barking excitedly alongside us.

"Are you going the right way?" Barney shouted.

"I don't know!" Suravi yelled again. She was in full yelling mode.

"This way!" Maika called, veering off to the right.

Maika seemed to know where she was going, so I pulled alongside her, ahead of the other two, panting and laughing. We ran past shops, past restaurants, past people staring at us suspiciously, catching glimpses of the sea in the distance as we went.

"Wait!" said Barney.

"Stop!" said Suravi.

We all slowed to a halt. Barney was clutching a stitch, Suravi couldn't speak, I was panting. Maika was dancing around like she could run for miles. She really liked her sports.

"Come on!" She pointed. "It's the tram, that funicular thing!"

We walked over to it, paid one pound twenty each, and climbed on board the little red and white box. After a few seconds it jolted and started easing us down the steep track. It sounded like a trolley being pushed down a corridor. We all crowded round the front window, staring out at the beach and the sea rippling away from us like an endless blue sheet, all creases and dimples. About thirty seconds later, we were there; we were standing on the sand.

"We've done it!" I said. "Phase One is complete!"

Suravi stared at me. "Phase One? What are you on about?"

I shrugged, awkward, feeling caught out.

"Phase One is getting here," I said, thinking fast. "Phase Two is getting back tomorrow."

Suravi frowned a bit, as if she wasn't buying it, but she didn't say anything.

"OK, now what?" asked Barney.

I pointed, as if they might not have noticed. "It's the sea!"

We started running again, feet sinking into soft sand. It was spitting with rain, but we didn't care – we dropped our bags, took our shoes and socks off, and splashed into the water. The tide was in, and a small wave broke over my feet, wetting my jeans. It was cold. Freezing cold.

Barney splashed me, so I kicked water back at him, and then we were all doing it, shouting and laughing, and Maika started singing "Sca-ah-borough" to the tune of "Hallelujah".

We walked back to the shore eventually and sat on the beach by our bags, exhausted. I dug my fingers into the sand and felt gritty grains slide under my fingernails. Milo was barking at the waves. I thought I could smell candy floss.

"Maybe we could stay here for ever," Maika said.

The beach stretched towards a lighthouse which sat on the harbour wall. It had four windows and I imagined living in it – looking out at this beach every day.

"Good idea," I said, agreeing with Maika for once. "Let's never leave."

Suravi and Barney both nodded.

In the end, though, we only stayed there for about another ten minutes, which is quite a bit less than for ever. We picked up our stuff and walked back up the cobbled slipway to the pavement.

"I'm hungry," said Barney.

"Shall we go to the flat before we get food, though?" asked Maika.

Suravi pointed. "I fancy *that*," she said.

She was looking at a black speedboat with gold stripes down the side. It was shaped like the pointy end of a spear, and it had black leather seats. Five pounds each for ten minutes.

"Water's a bit choppy," Barney said.

"All the better!" I told him.

"No." He shook his head firmly, frowning. "Don't think so."

I knew that frown. Sometimes Barney just wasn't up for something and there was nothing you could do to persuade him. Suravi and Maika tried, but they couldn't change his mind, so he waited on the quay, looking a bit sad, to be honest. We walked up to the guy, paid our money and got in the boat. I was aware of my funds depleting but I was pretty sure I still had enough for a taxi on Sunday evening. That was all I needed.

The man stood at the front by a small steering wheel.

"Hold on," he grunted.

We puttered away from the quay and I waved at Barney. Suddenly the engine roared, the front of the boat lifted up off the water, and we were speeding out across the bay.

The boat zoomed over a wave, it was in the air for a moment, then it bumped down into the trough behind it, soaking us in a great splash of spray that glittered like a rainbow.

"We're all going to drown!" Suravi laughed, and the boat screeched into a tight turn, making us all fall into each other. The driver must have enjoyed our screams of delight, because he swerved left and right, soaking us in spray. I gasped and yelled. This was exactly what I wanted – this buzzy feeling in my stomach and my chest. This was the complete opposite of carrying on as normal. The waves flexed and crested as we dropped and climbed, and salty water kept spattering into my face.

We came back to the quay and staggered off the boat towards Barney, feeling like we'd been on some wild rollercoaster.

"Good?" he said.

"Brilliant," I said, grinning.

"OK." He smiled back. "But I'm officially starving now."

Maika told us the flat was just a ten-minute walk, so we set off. It was near Marine Road, above the North Bay. We headed up a steep path, and after a while we turned on to a residential street lined by big, grimy houses.

Soon we could relax in Maika's friend's flat and have a takeaway.

"Turns out running away's easy," Suravi said. "We should do it more often."

"Milo!" Barney yelled. "Milo, no!"

The unruly ball of reddish-brown hair had suddenly yanked the lead out of Barney's hand. A startled cat disappeared round a corner, Milo hot on its heels.

We all rushed after him, shouting his name, yelling "Come back!" and waving our arms, but Milo veered off round another corner and out of sight. He's a shaggy little terrier with pointy ears and a pink tongue that always seems to be hanging out, as I mentioned before, but it was the short legs I was thinking about as we sprinted to the corner. How could he move so fast?

"Come back!" I yelled again.

Barney wailed frantically, "Milo!"

Suravi and Maika shouted his name too as we reached the corner and stopped abruptly, bumping into each other. No sign of him. The road stretched away, a load of side streets leading off it. Nothing to see but parked cars and houses. He'd totally vanished.

"No, no, no," Barney moaned. "Where is he?" He sounded desperate.

"Hey," I panted, breathless. I put my hand on his arm. "It's OK."

He turned on me, furious. "It's not OK!"

"All right, don't panic, we'll split up again." Suravi said. "Let's get into pairs. We'll find him, don't worry, we'll find him."

"We're right outside the house, by the way," Maika murmured.

It was a terrace of tall old houses with steps leading up to front doors. They'd all been split into flats; there were about six bells by each door. They looked nice. I wondered if we'd get a view of the sea...

Focus, Jasper. We had to find Milo.

A man wearing the top half of a grey suit with a blue shirt and jeans came out of one of the side streets. Milo was trotting along beside him on his lead. He saw us and barked and tried to run towards Barney, but the man yanked the lead, heading down another street.

Barney started running and yelling at the same time. "Hey, wait, that's my dog! Wait!"

The man turned and saw us all running towards him, shouting and waving our arms like we'd lost our minds. For a moment it looked like he was wondering what to do. Was he going to ignore us, just walk away? But he didn't move, he waited for us.

"Your animal?" he said, as Barney skidded to a halt in front of him.

"Yes!" Barney's face was lit up like it was Christmas Day. "Thank you, thank you, thank you!" He crouched down by Milo, picked him up and hugged him, calling him a "bad boy" while stroking and patting and wrestling with him, which was definitely sending mixed messages.

"I was about to phone the number on the collar," the man said. He had short grey hair and flushed pink skin. Small eyes, no chin. His face was basically flat.

"Thank you," I said.

"You should be more careful," he continued. He had a sharp, nasal voice and he stared at us curiously. "Where are you off to, anyway?"

Suravi stepped in. I knew she would. There was something grating about his manner.

"Not really any of your business," she said. "But thanks for finding him. Bye."

It was a bit rude, but at least she hadn't got her ninja throwing star out.

We all turned away and Maika led us to the front door. As she searched in her bag for the keys, Flat Face came up behind us. He was just standing there with his hands behind his back, watching us, like a creepy teacher.

"Well," he said creepily, "this is a coincidence."

Maika glanced over her shoulder at him, then found the key and opened the door. "Come on," she said. "Let's get inside."

We all shuffled through the door and I started to close it, but Flat Face put a hand out and stopped me.

"What are you doing?" I said, trying not to sound nervous.

He grinned at me, showing off very white teeth. "I live here." He followed us into the hallway. "Now, why don't you tell me what *you're* doing?"

I stared at him, genuinely confused. "What d'you mean? *We're* staying here."

His grey eyebrows pinched together and his small eyes got even smaller. "But you seem a bit jumpy? Everything all right?"

"We're fine," I said. "Just pleased to be here." I turned my back on him and climbed the stairs after my friends.

He followed us, climbing the stairs behind me. "That's nice – what have you got planned?"

He was probably trying to be friendly, but the questions just kept coming. "Don't know," I said, without turning round.

There were a lot of stairs. The flat was on the third floor. There was a musty smell, like the inside of a cardboard box. We all crowded on to the landing as Maika found a new key on her keyring. I turned round and stared at Flat Face, who'd followed us all the way.

"Anyway, thanks for finding Milo," I said again. "Bye."

"You don't live here," he told us, as if we might not know.

"My friend does," Maika said.

He stared at us: Suravi glaring at him, Maika stony-faced, Barney, who was avoiding his eye, and me probably looking unsettled.

"Well, if you need anything at all," he said, "let me know." He nodded, like he was agreeing with himself. "I'll keep an eye on you." He tapped a finger under his eye, as if he was pointing at it. I couldn't tell if he was trying to be reassuring or if he was warning us.

"Yeah, thanks," Suravi said. "We know where your eye is."

Flat Face took a key out of his pocket and unlocked the

door right across the landing from ours. *Oh, perfect.* He was basically living a few feet away.

Maika got our door open.

Flat Face turned back towards us, like he wanted the last word, but we all bundled into the flat and I slammed the door closed.

I leant against the wall. Suravi laughed. Barney said, "Bloody hell," and Maika said, "What a creep."

"Shh," I said. "He's probably still out there, listening."

"So what?" Suravi said loudly. "He's definitely a creep!"

Barney sniggered nervously. "'I'll keep an eye on you,'" he said in an exaggerated deep voice.

Maika led us through a little hallway into a big high-ceilinged room. It was a sitting room, with a green sofa, a green armchair and a long wooden table close to a window which took up most of one wall. I moved towards the window, leant my hands on the glass and squashed my nose against it. I could see the whole of North Bay stretching round to Peasholm Park and the Sea Life Centre. The dark sea was wrinkling like a restless creature, scribbled with white foam, and the pale blue sky above it was scribbled with white cloud.

"Look at the view!" I said. "This place is brilliant!" I was completely forgetting for a moment about, one, Flat Face; two, the police; three, lying to my parents and my friends; and in fact four, the whole reason we were here.

"This room's bigger than our garden," Barney

muttered, which was true, because his house basically doesn't have a garden.

Suravi had her arms out and she was spinning round, looking up at the high ceiling. "It's amazing," she said. "The journey gets four stars, but this place gets a solid five." She looked at Maika. "When I'm a millionaire, I might buy it off your mum's friend."

"You haven't seen the bedrooms yet," Maika told us, with a pleased grin, like she owned the place.

There were two, one with a double bed, one with two singles.

"Me and Jasper get the single beds!" Barney said.

"Whoa." Suravi had both her hands in the air. "Who says? Maika got us this flat, so we should get first choice."

"But Jasper has cancer!" Barney blurted.

Silence.

"I mean, he's not wrong," I said eventually, and we all laughed. It had been a bit of a day, and there was definitely some tension between us in need of a release.

"Let's toss for it," Maika said.

"If I lose, I'm downgrading this place to four stars," Suravi muttered.

She tossed a coin, I shouted "Heads!", Suravi dropped it and we all crowded round it on the floor.

It was tails.

"Ha!" Suravi cried, doing a little victory dance. "Five stars after all!"

We could have gone back down to the sea, but we were all knackered. We slumped on the soft green sofa and no one said anything for about one full minute.

Then my stomach rumbled loudly.

"Let's eat!" said Suravi.

ELEVEN

I hardly ever get a takeaway. Chicken Kiev from the supermarket was a treat because my parents are usually all about home cooking, so I was definitely up for a Chinese. I ordered salt and pepper squid, Barney picked roast duck in plum sauce, and we tried each other's. I also had a bit of Suravi's chicken with black bean sauce, but I wasn't interested in Maika's vegetable noodle thing. There was loads of egg fried rice and prawn crackers, too. I wanted a beer but couldn't be bothered with the hassle of trying to buy one so I got 7 Up instead, which is actually a good drink with Chinese – I heartily recommend it. Barney likes Lilt and that's not bad either. My mouth was all salt-and-peppery and a bit sweet and sticky too, so a long gulp of cold lemony 7 Up was perfect.

"I love Chinese!" Barney shouted.

"Me too!" I shouted back.

We were shouting because "Rain on Me" was playing really loudly on Suravi's phone. I took another mouthful of salty squid, then explained to her why Coke was the wrong drink for a Chinese meal. I was holding a prawn cracker in one hand and a forkful of duck in plum sauce in the other; she was laughing at me and sort of dancing in her chair and singing along and eating all at the same time. I thought this was definitely inching towards a Perfect Moment.

But then the table caught fire.

I was waving the prawn cracker and Suravi was waving her hands back at me, holding her knife and fork, and there was a tall white candle between us, which was nice. Maika had found it.

"All right, don't stab me!" I shouted, because her knife was getting a bit close to my face.

And then one of us – I reckon she did it, but she thinks I did it – knocked the candle over on to a pile of napkins that had come with the takeaway, and suddenly there were flames. Milo barked really loudly, Maika shouted, "Fire!", Suravi cackled hysterically, Barney yelped. The music was still blaring. I just yelled, "Water, water!" like a total fool.

Suravi grabbed my 7 Up, screeching, "Don't panic!" and poured it over the flames, but there was hardly any 7 Up left, and now the tablecloth was on fire too. We all jumped up and I was shouting, "It's all right!" and Barney was shouting, "No, it's not!" Suravi shoved a chair aside and poured more almost empty drinks over the flames and flapped at them with a plate, which didn't help even a little bit. By now pretty much the whole surface of the table was on fire.

Maika meanwhile had run to the kitchen. She came back with a jug of water, yelled, "Look out!" and chucked it on to the flames.

They hissed and went out, leaving a slimy black mess and a sour smoky damp smell. Suravi switched the music off, and suddenly it was very quiet. We all stared at the mess.

"All right, everyone," Maika said, "calm down. We're OK. Everything's OK."

There was a loud hammering at the door.

I jumped, Barney flinched, we all looked at each other.

"Who's that?" Barney whispered.

Another loud bang at the door.

"I bet I know," Suravi said.

No one was moving, so I went to open the door, putting the chain on first.

I saw a blue shirt, grey hair, a flat pink face.

"I heard yelling," our creepy neighbour said in his naggy nasal voice. "Everything all right?"

"Everything's fine. Thanks, though," I said, my words tumbling over each other. "Everything's totally fine. Bye!" I tried to close the door, but his foot was in it.

"Perhaps I should talk to an adult."

"She's not here," I blurted.

"Who's not here?"

"She's gone out. Could you move your foot, please? Just move it, please. Thanks."

I was definitely starting to sound a bit panicky. He just stood there, not moving his foot, doing a one-eyed stare through the narrow gap like he literally didn't believe a single word I'd said to him. Which was fair enough, because not a single word I'd said to him was true. If this continued much longer, I thought Suravi would probably march up behind me and start calling him names, and I didn't want that. I just wanted to close the door and get back to our evening.

"Anyway…" I said.

A few long seconds passed before he finally moved his foot. I slammed the door.

Then my phone rang. It was Mum. This definitely didn't feel like running away: too many adults involved. I was tempted to ignore the call, but I knew she'd just worry if I did that, so I answered.

"Hi, Mum!" I said. "Everything's totally fine!" I was trying to sound happy and relaxed, like we hadn't just nearly burned down the flat, and we weren't being stalked by our creepy neighbour, and the police weren't looking for us.

"Are you OK, Jasper?"

So I probably didn't get the tone quite right, because she immediately sensed something was wrong, in that

101

telepathic way that Mums do. I slid my back down the door and sat on the floor, leaning against it.

"I'm great," I told her. "Everything's totally fine!"

I winced – even *I* could hear that wasn't very convincing. So I kept talking. I told her we were in the middle of a brilliant Chinese takeaway, I was having salt and pepper squid, and the flat was lovely, she should see the view. I generally tried to steamroll her with a long, garbled stream of good news.

"I'm so glad, sweetheart," she said finally, sounding reassured. "That all sounds lovely. Well, I'll leave you to your Chinese, then. I checked trains; there's a direct one leaving at 4:07 tomorrow. That works, doesn't it?"

I stared at my phone for a moment. "Yes," I said after too much of a pause. "That works. That's perfect."

There was a pause at Mum's end too. I was basically holding my breath at this point, not sure if I'd sounded reassuring or if she was going to do the Mum telepathy thing.

"Right, well, maybe I'll call again tomorrow," she said finally. "Have a lovely evening, then. We miss you. See you tomorrow."

"OK!"

"Love you, chickpea."

"Love you back!" I said. "Bye."

I put the phone down and banged my head gently against the door, waves of guilt washing over me.

*

I'd brought "Pass the Pigs". It's a game where there's little pigs which are like dice and you throw them and get points. We played it to see who would do the washing up and who would do the clearing away. I got a Double Razorback, which was brilliant, but then on my very next throw the pigs were Making Bacon, so I got zero points. Suravi lost too, so we ended up in the small kitchen with a pile of plates, glasses and cutlery.

I was washing, she was drying. I don't see the point of drying – just put it on the drainer and leave it – but anyway. I had my hands in a sink full of hot, bubbly water. I actually don't mind a bit of washing up. Mountains of white bubbles, blue cloth, soapy lemon smell. It's quite calming. Although the water was too hot and my hands were turning red. I showed them to Suravi.

"Look," I said. "Red hands."

She just stood there, staring at me.

"What?" I said.

She picked up a plate and started giving it a really good dry with a tea towel which had a picture of Scarborough castle on it. She had her lips stuck out a bit, like she was thinking about a maths problem.

She stopped drying the plate. "You told me on the train you're OK," she said. "*Are* you?"

"No," I told her. "Red hands!"

She just stared at me again, her mouth crumpling up

impatiently. "You know, you can talk to me," she said. "About anything."

I glanced at her, then looked back at the bubbles. "I'm all right."

She tilted her head. "But you're not, are you? This must be a bit horrible. And scary."

Earlier, I'd felt like we'd almost had a Perfect Moment. It was nice, but the problem with chasing Perfect Moments was that Option Three meant I might never actually reach one. Maybe I was meant to have one in a year or two, or when I was twenty-three or thirty-seven or something, but I might never get there.

I found a knife under the water, took it out and wiped it with the cloth.

"I was thinking," I said. "I want to call it Steve."

She stared at me. "What?"

"I never feel like saying, you know, 'cancer' or 'tumour'. So let's call it Steve instead."

She nodded. "OK."

There was a window above the sink, but it was so dark outside you couldn't see anything. "Because Steve was that boy – remember? – who left and went down south," I said. "And he was a jerk."

Suravi nodded. "I remember. And your cancer's a jerk, and it's going to leave and go down south. Sort of."

"It's not *my* cancer," I said. Although, even as I said it, I thought maybe it was. I gave her the knife. She dried it.

"We don't have to talk about it if you don't want to," she told me.

I looked at the bubbles again. "I don't know what's worse, talking about it or not talking about it."

After that, neither of us said anything for a bit. I washed two more plates and another knife.

"I wish I could throw a chair at it," I said eventually, remembering her epic chair toss in the canteen. "At Steve. Or I wish I could fight it the same way you fought Joe Hancock."

That was legendary. Joe Hancock's a year older than us, and he looks like an American footballer. I mean, he's *really* big. Way back in Year 7 he started picking on Suravi, and one day she flew at him like a guided missile, all fists and knees. He was doubled up and bleeding from his mouth before he shoved her away and she fell into a door. They both got excluded.

So yeah, if I could throw a chair at Steve, or attack it, that would feel pretty good. It would be satisfying and I'd be doing something, rather than just standing around uselessly with this disease inside me. But the thing is, you don't fight cancer, you just have it. Even when the treatment started, I was just going to be lying there, feeling sick, while doctors and nurses did things to me. There was nothing for me to actually *do*, no part for me to play, except to be looked after like a houseplant. And then possibly still finish up with Option Three.

"I think the reason this trip felt like a good idea," I said, "is that I'm actually *doing* something. Not even getting away from anything, not really, but *doing* something."

"Yeah." Suravi nodded. "I get that."

I glanced at her. "Thanks for coming," I said. "It's really nice of you."

She smiled. "I'm your mate, aren't I? Ever since cheese muffins in Year 3." She wasn't looking at me any more, she was staring at a plate she was drying, but it was nice all the same. Girls are much better at serious talks than boys. They just are. "But there's another reason why I was up for getting out of town." She hesitated. She was turning the plate round and round. "They're maybe going to kick me out of school."

I stared at her. "Seriously?"

She nodded. "Turns out they don't like it when you throw a chair at a teacher."

"But you didn't!" I squeaked. "You said yourself – you just threw it, sort of *towards* her."

She shrugged. "They don't care about the details. They've got this whole file on me going back to Year 7. Robinson showed it to me. It's about this thick." Her finger and thumb were like three inches apart.

She was definitely exaggerating, but it was the wrong time to question it. I shook my head. "That sucks."

"You know that I sometimes just lose it." Her tone was sad but cool, like she was talking about someone else. "I feel this anger building up and building up and I'm thinking, 'Calm down,' but I can't calm down, and suddenly there's this rage and I'm doing something I'm going to regret. Apparently, I lack 'impulse control'."

I had bits of irrelevant cutlery in my hands, so I put them down and wrapped my arms round her shoulders. It was an awkward hug, because she was still holding the plate, and because we don't usually do hugging, but it was still nice. I stepped back.

"By the way," I said, "I think Barney likes you."

She smiled. "He's only human."

I smiled too. "OK. But let him down gently."

After that, we went back into the sitting room. Maika and Barney had thrown away the burnt tablecloth and the slimy ashes. The big window was open, so it didn't smell too bad. The sky was huge, dark and full of stars.

I flopped on to the sofa.

I'd thought that running away with friends (yeah, OK, Maika too) would mean having fun and basically laughing the whole time. But it wasn't like that. I felt gloomy because I was ill, and apparently Suravi might get expelled, and I used to be mates with Maika but I wasn't any more, and Barney was a bit low generally and I didn't know why.

They'd all been pretty keen to run away – Barney had come up with the idea, Suravi had insisted it was possible, Maika had offered the flat. And now I realized that maybe they all had their own stuff they were running away from.

"Oi!" Two hands clapped my cheeks. I turned. "Don't be sad," Barney said. "We're here to have a laugh. Beach tomorrow, and arcades, and ice cream."

"Be sad if you want," said Suravi, "but be happy too, cos look, it's us, we're all here!"

"Yes," said Maika. "We're in this together."

I smiled at them all, even Maika. I mean we obviously weren't in it together, because I was ill and they weren't; I was going to find Uncle Universe and they were going to go home; I was staring down the barrel of Option Three and they weren't. But still – here I was with my friends in Scarborough, in this brilliant flat, in a room with a tall window full of the night sky.

OK, it wasn't a Perfect Moment for various reasons, but I remembered the doctor in her office, telling us the news, and I thought about how lonely I'd been feeling ever since, and I suddenly had a lump in my throat, because I felt like I'd do anything for my friends. (Except Maika.)

"I want to show you something," Maika said.

Their bedroom, the one with the twin beds, had a sloping ceiling with two skylights, one high up, and one lower. Maika shoved a bed over a bit, climbed up on to it, and pushed the lower skylight open.

"What are you doing?" asked Suravi.

Maika didn't answer. She just climbed out on to the roof.

TWELVE

"Wait!" said Barney. "Careful!"

Too late. Maika had bounced off the bed and pulled herself up through the skylight. Her knees, ankles and feet disappeared and then she was gone. The whole manoeuvre took about two seconds flat.

There was a moment's pause, and then her face appeared.

"Come on up!" she said.

Suravi laughed. "OK, then."

She jumped on to the bed, reached up to the edges of the skylight, bounced and pulled, kicking her feet like a short ballet dancer, and disappeared through the hole.

I looked at Barney. "We better follow them," I said.

He shook his head, frowning. "No. Not me. Your shed roof? Fine. But I'm definitely not doing this."

I was already getting on the bed. I saw the frown, but I

still tried to persuade him. "Oh, come on!" I said. "Why not? You might impress Suravi."

He looked at me, so I shrugged. "You're interested in her, right?"

He snorted. "I don't think falling off the roof and dying is going to make a good impression."

I started to say something else, I didn't even know what, but I just liked the idea of all four of us being up there together. He interrupted me.

"Seriously," he said, "why would I? Why is climbing out on the roof about fifty feet up in the sky, where if you slide off you'll definitely splat on the pavement and *die...*" He took a breath, suddenly realizing what he was saying and looking sideways at me. "I just mean, why is that a good idea?"

I stood on the bed, unsteady, looking at him. Barney gets nervous easily. He's always been scared of stuff. Quite often I think that's a bit of a shame, because it means he misses out, like he did with the speedboat. But I could see his point in this case.

"Yeah," I said. "I actually can't argue with that."

But I still reached up to the edges of the skylight, bounced and pulled. I hooked my elbows on to the roof and slithered clumsily out on to the tiles. Because Barney was probably right – it absolutely makes sense to stay safely on your bed and look up at the skylight, but sometimes I think it's good to climb through it anyway.

And then I was three floors up, basically sitting in the actual sky. It was only a shallow slope from the skylight down towards the long drop to the street, but all the same I crept carefully upwards, away from the edge, to join Maika and Suravi.

"Used to come out here with my sister when we stayed here," Maika said. "Pretty nice, isn't it?"

It was amazing. The tiles were still warm from the day's sun. They were rough and uneven under my fingers and smelled dusty. There was a light, cool breeze on my face, and there was a view over the roofs and out to sea, far out to sea, where a light on a ship was blinking way out there on the dark water. I stared at the view for a while and then lay down flat on the roof and looked up. Stars and stars and stars, like freckles gone wild.

Milo barked in the bedroom below us. "You guys all right?" we heard Barney shout.

I looked at Suravi and Maika, who both had dreamy smiles on their faces as they gazed up into the night.

"Yeah," I shouted back. "We're good!"

We were good. I wanted to spend the whole night out there, go to sleep on the roof. Climbing through the skylight felt like taking a big step away from real life. *This* felt like running away. Maybe I didn't just want to spend the night out here, maybe I wanted to live out here. Stay on the roof for ever. Or I could split my time between here and the lighthouse on the beach.

111

At that moment I felt like running away was the best idea I'd ever had. Or, to be fair, that Barney had ever had.

I heard barking again; it was loud and distressed. I sat up.

"Is that Milo?" I asked.

Suravi shook her head. "It's on the street."

We inched down the roof and peered carefully over the edge. It was scary to look down – it made me feel a bit dizzy, but the street lights were lit and I could see the pavement on the opposite side of the road. Someone was approaching a dirty red van parked in a pool of yellow light. With one hand he was clutching a dog that was wriggling and barking desperately, with the other he was holding a phone.

"I'm dropping this one off on the way," he was saying, his voice clear and sharp in the quiet street. "Be with you in half an hour. Pour me a Jameson."

It was our creepy, flat-faced neighbour.

"What's he doing?" I whispered.

He opened the back of his van, chucked the dog in, then slammed it shut.

"Who cares?" whispered Maika.

She and Suravi shuffled back up the roof, away from the edge.

She had a point. Who cared if he wasn't very nice to his dog? It was a bit odd, though. When we first met him, it had looked like he was just walking off with Milo. The dog was still barking in the back of the van as he jumped in and drove way.

I was still leaning forward, craning my neck towards the street, when Barney's head suddenly poked out of the skylight behind me. "What's going on?" he said. He made me jump and I gasped as I lost my grip on the tiles. All of a sudden I was sliding towards the edge, towards the gutter, towards the fifty-foot drop where if you slide off you'll definitely splat on the pavement and die.

I yelled and threw a hand backwards. I kept yelling and I kept sliding, and I was pretty sure I was about to die. Someone grabbed my hand, but our fingers tangled and parted and I was still sliding. My feet went right out over the edge of the roof, but whoever it was grabbed my wrist just as I kicked wildly at the slippery gutter and got one foot jammed in it.

I stopped sliding.

I stopped yelling.

I just lay there, splayed out across the roof, not daring to move at all, gasping and panting, my whole body rigid, wondering if I'd actually peed my pants.

Stars and stars and stars up above me, all cold and far away and not caring that I'd nearly died, that I still might die. It turned out the roof wasn't such a brilliant place after all.

I twisted my head slowly, slowly, and looked behind me. Barney's shocked face was frozen in the skylight. Up above him, Maika was gripping my wrist, gritting her teeth. "Hang on!" she gasped. She had her knees bent, feet flat on the roof, and she was leaning backwards. I kept my right foot jammed in the gutter and bent my left leg, foot flat on the roof like Maika's, and I pushed.

"Wait!" said Suravi. She reached down and got hold of my wrist too, and she and Maika both pulled.

"We got you," Suravi panted.

"Shuffle towards us!" Maika said.

"I am shuffling!" I snapped.

Slowly, slowly, I moved back up the roof, away from the edge.

"Oh, that was very, very bad," I muttered. "So bad, so bad."

As soon as I was next to the skylight, I slid through it, wanting to be off the roof – off the roof and never ever back on it again. I dropped on to the bed and lay there, shaking a bit, clutching the duvet like it might be about to fly away, muttering, "So bad, so bad."

Milo and Barney just stared at me, and Maika and Suravi's faces appeared in the skylight above me, also staring.

I expected Barney to say, *I told you so*, but he didn't, he put a reassuring hand on my shoulder and said, "You're all right, mate. Take your time – you're OK."

Milo jumped up on the bed beside me and licked my cheek.

And then Maika and Suravi fell on the bed next to me, and Maika said, "We basically saved your life."

And Suravi said, "It's true – we're heroes."

I started to laugh then, a kind of grim chuckle, and finally sat up. I took a deep breath in, and then let a long, quivering breath out.

"Thank you," I said. "Thank you for saving my life."

We found some hot chocolate, and we all had one to calm ourselves down. It wasn't great, because we had to make it with water (we had no milk), but it helped. It was hot and sweet and I burnt my tongue a bit.

Suravi, Maika and I squashed on to the green sofa and Barney and Milo sat on the green armchair as we noisily sipped our drinks. I cupped mine in both hands as if it was chilly, which it wasn't.

"Well," Suravi said, "that was a day."

"It was an amazing day … with some scary parts," said Barney. He counted them off on his fingers: "I didn't enjoy losing Maika, losing Milo, and nearly losing Jasper."

"Maybe amazing days with scary parts are the best types of day?" Maika murmured.

We were all quiet for a minute while we thought about it. And then we pretty much all said "No!" at once, so we laughed.

"Definitely not that last part," I said.

And then we went to bed. I was really tired after not

115

sleeping well last night, and the last couple of days had been hard work in lots of ways, but still, I had trouble getting to sleep. My whole body was jangling with nerves like a bell that's just been hit really hard. Every now and then I'd shiver uncontrollably and my stomach would lurch, as if I was falling and about to go splat on the pavement.

Also, less importantly – but still importantly – I wasn't used to sharing a bed with Barney. We'd put a pillow between us and his head was down the other end of the bed, but still, he kept rolling around in his sleep and he was breathing heavily. Every now and then he'd sort of snort and make a noise that was almost like snoring but not quite.

Plus, of course, I was worrying about what would happen the next day. Phase Two of running away, which I'd been trying not to think about, was suddenly really close. I was going to have to tell Suravi, Barney and Maika that, in fact, I wasn't going home with them.

And then they'd get on the train and leave, and I'd be alone.

Which was a bit worrying.

So there was all that, and my shoulder was throbbing.

I touched it lightly. The lump under my T-shirt. Steve. It was warm and sore, and it didn't belong there. I thought about Option Two, radical surgery, which meant losing my arm. I tried to imagine waking up in hospital with a bit of me missing. People would feel sorry for me, girls probably wouldn't be interested in me, I wouldn't be able to tie my own shoelaces. I wondered if phantom limb pain was a real thing and what it would feel like. All of that was bad, but then there was Option Three, which was even worse. I didn't want to think about those things, but I couldn't help it.

I quietly got out of the bed, fetched a long cushion from the sofa, put it on the floor by the bed and lay on that. I squashed my pillow under my head.

And I still didn't feel quite right.

So I rolled off the long cushion on to my back, then shimmied right under the bed. I took my pillow with me. This was better. It was dusty and the carpet was scratchy, and it smelled like old people. It wasn't actually comfortable at all, but it was still, somehow, better. I lay on my back and ran my finger along the wooden slats inches above my face. I felt safe under here. It was probably a bit weird, like climbing into my mum's wardrobe would have been weird, but I didn't care because I felt safe.

But I still couldn't sleep. I was just lying there, not sleeping, on the floor under the bed. And the floor was very hard and my shoulder was still throbbing.

There was too much going on inside my head. I needed to take my mind off the floor and my shoulder, to avoid thinking about falling, to distract myself from Barney almost snoring, and to try my best not to think about my friends going home tomorrow and being left alone.

So I thought about Uncle Universe instead, him sitting by my bed when I was little, coming up with a whole world that he just plucked out of nowhere. I tried to remember what happened next in Oswaldhover after Jasper fell into the sky. There was definitely an alien who came along in a sort of flying rowing boat, and he took Jasper away. That much I could remember.

I fell asleep eventually and dreamt that I was being taken somewhere, but I had no idea where I was going.

SUNDAY

THIRTEEN

I was cold and achy when I woke up and my dream was stuck in my head: that unsettling sense that I didn't know where I was going. I wriggled out carefully from under the bed like a soldier avoiding sniper fire and sat up, stretching my arms above my head and yawning. Barney had propped up his pillow and he was reading (of course) and scratching Milo (of course), who was sitting on his chest and occasionally licking his cheek. He lets his iguana sit on his chest too. He likes animals, Barney. You know where you are with animals.

He looked at me. "What you doing down there?" he asked. He had his usual good-natured smile on his face, but there was a little twist of concern in his lips. Which actually is also standard for him.

"Slept on the floor," I told him. "Clearly."

Barney nodded and turned back to his book. It *looked*

like he was reading, but he whispered, like he was talking to himself, "That was really scary, on the roof."

I sat on the floor, looking up at him. "Yeah, it was a bit."

Barney was still staring at his book. "I think it's OK to be scared," he said in that same quiet voice. And then he looked up from his book, finally, and looked straight at me. "Cos why should you have to be brave if you don't feel like it?"

I was pretty sure that Barney wasn't talking about the roof any more, he was talking about Option Two and Option Three … and maybe about himself too.

"Yeah," I told him. "I think you're right."

Milo lifted his head and pointed his nose at me. Then he jumped off Barney's chest and jumped into my lap. I gave him a good scratch and a pat.

I thought about how Barney was scared of everything, including speedboats. And yet he'd been the one to suggest running away in the first place.

Neither of us said anything for a bit, but before it could get awkward, Barney announced, "I'm hungry!" and this time he wasn't doing a quiet voice at all, he was doing it like it was a proper, important announcement.

We staggered out of our room to look for breakfast. The girls' bedroom door was closed, so we left them to sleep. We found bread in the freezer and sat down at the table with three slices of toast each. I had two with peanut butter and the third with peanut butter and marmalade.

Neither of us said anything for a bit, we just ate. "So yeah," said Barney eventually, his mouth full of his second slice. He glanced at the girls' bedroom door. "I'm interested in Suravi. What about you and Maika?"

I stared at him. "What?"

He swallowed his toast and smiled. He picked up his third slice and waved it at me. "I always thought there was something there," he told me, eyebrows raised. "Something going on with you two."

I made a sceptical face, but the memory of me and Maika in the field, leaning against each other, laughing, came into my head. The image of her walking into my garden, looking like an athlete.

"Maybe once," I said. "Before … you know … everything."

And then I turned away, holding my toast, to look at the bookshelves. I'd had enough of that conversation. Barney unpacked a sachet of dog food and a bowl for Milo, and I found a folded-up map of the local area with "EXPLORER" written across it in big capitals. I didn't actually want to explore, I was just going to get a taxi from Scarborough to Robin Hood's Bay where I was hoping Uncle Universe still lived, but I took the map off the shelf and started to unfold it. The squashed little map on my phone had told me there was something called the Cleveland Way connecting Scarborough and Robin Hood's Bay, but I wanted an overview.

Before I could have a look, though, Barney dug some money out of his pocket and slammed it on the table.

"Let's see how much cash we've got for the day," he said. "I've got a tenner spending money from my parents, plus the eleven sixty I had already. Minus the stuff I bought in York, plus the busking money. How much have you got?"

I got out my money. After what I'd spent on waffles in York, and the speedboat, I had twelve pounds fifty-six left. I didn't want to spend any more of it, I wanted to save it for when they'd all gone. I needed to start making plans for that, because in just a few hours I was going to be on my own. And what if Uncle Universe wasn't even at that address any more? Or what if he was at the address but didn't want to see me? Where would I sleep? What would I do? Would I call my parents?

The closer I got to being on my own, the more I suspected that the plan I'd proudly thought wasn't ridiculous might in fact be slightly ridiculous after all. I was going to be an adult soon, if I avoided Option Three. I should probably start trying to be a rational adult.

The girls came into the kitchen, wearing dressing gowns they'd found last night which swamped them. Suravi was yawning, Maika was scratching her head. Suravi's hair flowed down over her shoulders in a black wave.

"Never seen your hair out of a braid," said Barney.

Suravi sort of shook her head around to show it off.

"Your lucky day," she told him. She looked at me. "You sleep all right? After the drama?"

I shrugged. "Reasonably."

"OK," she said, "I'm ready for breakfast. Who's going to be Mum?"

"I always have scrambled eggs on Sundays," Maika said.

"I can do scrambled eggs and bacon!" said Barney. "But we haven't got any eggs. Or bacon."

"I'll get them," I said, "but only if someone else cooks, cos I can't cook."

Suravi nodded happily. "Barney's volunteered. Barney's a star."

Barney grinned and seemed to stand up a little straighter.

I wasn't keen on spending my money, but I figured they'd pay me back for most of it, and I didn't mind getting the stuff because I wanted to be outside again, reminding myself I was in Scarborough, miles and miles away from all my problems. I dived into the bathroom for a quick wash, pulled on a T-shirt and jeans, and then, on impulse, took Uncle Universe's letter out of my bag and shoved it in my pocket. I tip-toed past our creepy neighbour's door. *Be with you in half an hour.* Where had he been going last night?

I shook my head to get him out of my mind, ran down three flights of stairs and heard seagulls squeaking and squealing as soon I pushed the front door open. I walked

125

right past the Tesco Express, round the corner and on to the road overlooking the bay.

I leant over the railings, like a figurehead on a ship, and breathed in deeply, forcing the salty smell right into my nostrils. Way down below me, the water was washing against the sea defences. OK, I was going to be a rational adult one day, hopefully, but for now I was at the seaside!

I lifted up my arms and opened my mouth wide. I wanted to shout my name as loud as I could … but there were still people around, so I just said it instead:

"Jasper."

And then I sort of half shouted it: "Jasper!"

Staring out at the sea, green and blue and blue and green all the way to the horizon. I felt like the breeze was filling me up, inflating me, so I might rise right off this hill and float away, like the Jasper in Uncle Universe's story.

There's much more water in the world than there is land. We learned that back in Year 6. Also, humans are about seventy-five per cent water (I mean, I don't remember the exact percentage, but we're definitely *mostly* water), so I reckon we must be naturally drawn to it. And who even knows what's in the ocean? It's about seven miles deep at its deepest point. You could put Mount Everest in there and still have plenty of room left over, and there are giant squid down there which are literally sea monsters. Staring out at the horizon, I loved the size of it and the mystery and magic of it. But not the cold of it. I was definitely going to have a swim later … probably … if I dared … but it would be icy, balls-freezingly cold.

I stood there a bit longer, gripping the railings, looking out at the green and blue and thinking about being here alone, without Suravi and Barney and Maika. I was going to have to tell them I'd been lying to them – that this whole trip was about finding Uncle Universe. And then I was going to stay here while they went home, which was another thing I wasn't sure about. But I was going to do it. Because I had to. I had to cut ties with everyone, leave it all behind. Basically, I wanted to control my own destiny.

For as long as I could, anyway.

I pulled Uncle Universe's letter out of my pocket. He'd sent it to me nine years ago, after he fell out with my mum. My grandma had just died, so I basically lost them both in the space of about a month. We'd been a family of five, and then suddenly there were only three of us. I remembered the gloom in the house, the quietness that seemed to last for weeks. Mum's tense, sad face. It felt like grandma and Uncle Universe had both died.

I took the letter out of the envelope and tried to smooth it out. It was delicate, a bit torn at the creases, and I handled it carefully. I didn't want it blowing away on a sea breeze. The handwriting was faded, the letters were small and they were all leaning forwards, as if they were being crushed by a weight, but they were clear enough.

Anything you need, <u>absolutely anything</u>, please come to me. I'll help, I promise. Because I'm magic!

I mean, it was pretty clear. When I knocked on his door, when I showed him his promise, he'd have to take me in.

I had about eight pounds left after I bought the milk, eggs and bacon. Probably not enough for a taxi to Robin Hood's Bay. I'd have to borrow some from Suravi or Barney, which would be an awkward conversation, but I was still OK. My plan was still on course.

When I got back, Maika was braiding Suravi's hair, and Barney was on the sofa with his book. He jumped up and got the bacon frying. Soon there were great smells coming from the kitchen. Maika ended up doing the eggs in a different pan, because she's vegetarian, and I put more toast in and put the kettle on. Suravi finished doing her hair. We sat down to our breakfast – or second breakfast for Barney and me – and talked about what we would do today.

"Beach," said Suravi. "Obviously."

"And arcades!" said Barney.

I was sliding toast and bacon round my plate, trying to scoop the last bit of scrambled egg on to it.

"D'you remember that school trip to Blackpool, when we were at Hazelwood?" said Maika, suddenly excited. "We made that sandcastle with the drawbridge, and the turrets—"

"And we found a bird's skull and we stuck it on top!" I said without even thinking about it. "Best sandcastle ever. That was brilliant." For a moment we were grinning at each other like we were best mates. Which was weird. Then we stopped.

She frowned. I looked away.

We started in the jangling, hazy light of an amusement arcade, among beat-'em-ups, shoot-'em-ups and racers, sticky carpets, the sweet smell of cleaning fluids and sweaty bodies. We swayed on motorbikes, sat inside twirling capsules, took each other on at an ancient *Street Fighter* machine. It turned out Maika was the queen of the beat-'em-ups. I was Ryu − a muscly guy in a sleeveless karate outfit and a red headband − and she was Blanka − a green beast with orange hair. She destroyed me, kicking, punching, head-butting and biting Ryu, until gobbets of blood flew around the screen.

Suravi provided a commentary: "She's kneed him in the face, she's jumped on his head, he can't do a thing about it. Now it's the electric shock … He can't take much more of this … Oh dear! She's cannonballed right into him − he's down, he's out, it's all over!"

Maika took her hands from the controls and shook them, blowing her fingertips. "In here, I'm invincible," she said.

Barney and Suravi were both laughing, and I could see

why, but it did make me think, just a little, of the fact that I'd ended up in hospital thanks to her.

We went to grab food, and I reminded them I'd bought breakfast, so they bought my fish and chips for me. Then we ran across the road to the beach and sat on the sand, facing the sea. I checked my money. I had less than a fiver now, thanks to mindlessly shoving pound coins in the machines in the arcades. It definitely wasn't enough for a taxi. But it wasn't a disaster. I could get a bus, or borrow some of theirs. I was still OK. I'd been having a good time, and I wanted to keep having a good time for as long as possible. Because I knew everything was going to change, very soon.

I had loads of salt and vinegar on my chips, and I burnt my tongue because I stuffed three of them in straight away. Then I had to brush grainy, sticky sand off my fingers or else I was going to end up eating half the beach. And it was still great. There aren't many things better than fish and chips.

Barney fed Milo a couple of chips, and I threw one up to a seagull the size of a Labrador which swooped, snatched it and wheeled away.

"There's something you feed seagulls," I said, "to make them explode. Can't remember what it is. Phosphorus?"

"Wouldn't that make them luminous?" asked Barney.

"Why do you want to make a seagull *explode*?" asked Suravi, outraged.

"I don't!" I protested. "I'm just saying."

I was watching the seagull flying away when I saw, or thought I saw, our creepy neighbour. He was standing next to a pirate who was advertising boat trips. He turned away abruptly, as if he'd seen me looking, and disappeared behind the queue waiting for the boat. Short grey hair, flat, pink face, now wearing blue jeans and a pale blue T-shirt – I was pretty sure it had been him. Was he watching us? Why would he do that?

Or maybe I just imagined it. I kept watching, but I didn't see him again. We finished our food and we chatted. The conversation slid and slipped around, moving into the past. It turned out we all had vivid memories of our primary school, Hazelwood.

"I will never not see you with your long, wobbly Mr Tickle arms!" said Suravi, pointing at me. They all started laughing at me, which made me laugh along with them. My mum had got the date of World Book Day wrong, and I'd turned up at school dressed as Mr Tickle. Seriously, it was years ago, but apparently they were never going to forget it.

"And it was only a bit after that when you decided to make cheese muffins with me," I said.

Suravi nodded. "I felt sorry for you."

Now Maika pointed at her. "Not true! You told me it was because you didn't know where to start and Jasper looked like he knew what he was doing!"

131

"Doesn't sound like Jasper," Barney said.

I turned to him. "OK, remember the Christmas play, when you forgot your line as a shepherd, and instead you announced that you'd had warmed up curry for breakfast? That was classic…"

We talked about Sports Days. The year the sack race ended in a massive pile-up of bodies halfway down the course. Me and Maika, the quickest in our year in the sprint, basically just racing each other. One year I'd win, the next year she'd win. We were competitive with each other, but I secretly never minded when she won. She'd be so happy she'd do a little victory dance on the finishing line.

It was weird how we all remembered Hazelwood so clearly. It definitely hadn't seemed like *that* much fun at the time, but now, part of me wished we were still there. Life was simpler in primary school.

We were all smiling again, and you could maybe have called this a Perfect Moment, but I didn't think it counted because it was all about the past. It almost felt like this conversation was actually happening in the past, it was yesterday already and this picnic on the beach was sliding backwards, becoming a half-remembered thing that we did ages ago.

Suravi pointed at me, grinning. "Talking of curry, remember when you and me and Maika had to make one in food tech, and it made Miss Brooks retch?"

I laughed. "Yes! That was only last year. It was just before—" And then I stopped. It was just before me and Maika fell out. Just before Maika started being horrible and I finished up with a broken wrist.

There was silence because we were all thinking about me and Maika falling out. And although we seemed to be getting better at silences, this one was uncomfortable.

"So anyway," said Barney after what felt like about a year and a half, "we going to swim, or what?"

We all had our costumes on under our clothes. We stripped off, made a big pile of clothes and towels and ran down to the water's edge. Barney paused with Milo.

"Go ahead," he said. "Maybe I'll come in after."

He and Milo stayed in the shallows while Suravi, Maika and I waded in deeper.

"Oh God, so cold, so cold!" I squealed, dancing around in the freezing water, which was just coming up to my trunks.

"This is a bad idea!" Suravi shrieked, also dancing. "This is a very bad idea!"

My legs were literally frozen, I was shivering all over, and when the water reached my balls I gasped and my entire body seemed to shrivel up.

Suravi started laughing hysterically, and Maika grimly waded forwards.

"Come on, you wimps!" she shouted.

"All right," I replied, "all right, here we go!"

I dived forwards, face first into the sub-zero sea, the salty water going up my nose and into my eyes, and for a moment I didn't have Steve and wasn't lying to my parents, I'd never fallen out with Maika, I wasn't being followed by a creepy neighbour, and I wasn't about to disappear, cutting myself off from everyone who loved me. It was just me and the cold, cold, freezing cold water.

I surfaced with a yell and Suravi immediately splashed me. Maika was on her back, kicking up water, and I did some kind of clumsy front crawl. Barney was watching us, ankle deep, with Milo sitting obediently behind him.

"Are you coming?" I shouted.

"Come on!" Maika yelled.

"It's really warm!" Suravi added, totally lying.

Barney hesitated, told Milo to stay, then grinned and started wading in, and I started to think that yes, this might finally be it, this might be an actual Perfect Moment.

But then I looked past Barney.

Milo was barking, and Barney was laughing and still wading towards us, but behind him, back up the beach, someone was rooting through our clothes.

FOURTEEN

I shouted at Barney, and he waved and laughed.

I pointed past him and yelled: "Our clothes!"

He looked confused, he shook his head and half lifted his arms, palms out, but finally he turned round, and then he saw what was happening. He sprinted back as I swam and splashed and waded as fast as I could for the shore, followed by Suravi and Maika. Milo got there first, skidding to a stop by the clothes and barking frantically at the figure.

The guy straightened up. I saw blue jeans and a pale blue T-shirt. A pink face. He glanced towards Barney running towards him, and then towards me, Suravi and Maika splashing out of the water, and he left. He didn't even run, he walked fast and then jogged, over the road and up a steep side street, out of sight.

It all happened quickly, and my eyes were full of salty

water, squinting into the sun, but I was sure it was him. It was Flat Face, our creepy neighbour.

We gathered round our clothes and checked our stuff. Our money was still there.

"What was he doing?" squeaked Barney.

No one answered, because no one knew.

"Weirdo," Suravi snapped.

We were all staring at the side street where he'd disappeared, as if we expected him to suddenly come back. We'd been having such a good time, and this man, this creepy guy, seemed to have decided randomly to make us feel unsafe and uncomfortable. He was like cancer. He was unwanted and he didn't belong, but he barged into my life anyway, making me miserable. He was probably called Steve. Well, I wasn't going to be miserable. I was planning on at least another happy hour or two before I told my friends I wasn't going home.

I rubbed my towel over my face, then lowered it. "Sandcastle?" I said.

Suravi looked at Barney. "We'll get ice creams." She said it in a firm way that meant he couldn't disagree with her. They pulled on T-shirts. "You two," she said, nodding at me and Maika, "while we're gone, are going to talk. About stuff."

And off they went. It was strange, being left so abruptly alone with Maika, but at least we had something to do with our hands. I drew a big circle in the sand with my finger, then we started digging out a moat and piling the dug-up sand in the middle.

Neither of us said anything for a while. The problem was, Suravi wanted us to talk, but I had no idea where to start. I was pretty sure that thing I'd told Barney – "It's gone way beyond talking" – was wrong, and probably also childish. I mean, if you don't talk, what are you left with? Sulking or glaring or fighting, none of which sounded good to me. I thought of my mum and Uncle Universe. It had gone way beyond talking with them too, whatever "it" was, and as a result we hadn't seen him for nine years and I really missed him, and I thought my mum probably did too.

So, fine, we should talk. But what should we say? There was sand under my fingernails and I was shivering a bit because I was still wet, and neither of us was speaking. The silence felt so awkward I almost wished Flat Face would come back.

I started wondering what was going through Maika's head. I didn't have to wonder for long, though. "I'm going to tell you," she said, not looking at me, digging out the moat, "why I was so angry with you last year."

Well, that was a different perspective for a start. She'd been *angry* with me?

"OK," I said, genuinely intrigued. I started building a wall between the mound and the moat. I wasn't looking at her, and she still wasn't looking at me. The tide was coming in. A tongue of water hissed over the sand and tickled my toes.

Maika stuck pebbles into the wall and started making a turret. I picked up a boiled sweet wrapper and stuck it on a long, thin shell. I pushed it into the top of the turret.

"You called me a 'nutter'," she said.

The sea reached the edge of the moat, then drew back, shushing over the pebbles. We dug the moat deeper. Grains of sand under my fingernails again.

"Did I?" I said.

She nodded. "Yes, you did."

The next tongue of seawater spilt right into the moat and soaked into the sand. It wasn't getting any less cold.

"And the thing is, I was… I was having a really rubbish time. My dad was long gone, Andi was at York, Mum was always working. I felt like my whole world was cracking into pieces and it was too much…" She hesitated, trying to find the words, then gave up. She shrugged. "It was just too much."

Another wave arrived. Maika went to her bag and got out the Barbie I'd seen when we were having lunch in York. She stuck it, feet first, arms raised in the air, into the top of our mound. The frilly, flowery dress ruffled in the breeze off the sea. Barbie stared at the approaching tide with a confident smile and cold eyes.

We stood side by side beside our sandcastle, behind our wall, not speaking, not looking at each other, and watched water splash into the moat. I was trying to think seriously about what she'd just said to me, but I didn't really get it.

"*It was too much.*" What did that mean?

I remembered Andi meeting Maika in York. "*You OK? You sure?*"

"I'm … sorry?" I said finally. It felt like that's what she wanted me to say. I almost shrugged, but I stopped myself, because Suravi wanted us to sort things out, and I wanted that too. But I just didn't get it.

Maika's face was all pinched and sad. "You don't sound sorry," she said quietly.

The way I remembered it, Maika picked on me for the last three months or so of Year 10. In the end she tripped me up on the stairs on the way up to French and I broke my wrist and ended up in hospital. After that, she stopped picking on me – she just ignored me. The sea was filling the moat, nudging and lapping at our wall. I was biting my lip. Was I supposed to forgive her for the way she'd been, and for the broken wrist because… Because she got stressed?

We were pressed up close to each other inside the wall, both looking out to the sea that was starting to surround us.

"You broke my wrist," I told her, like she didn't know.

Maika finally looked at me. "I didn't mean to do that!" she said, sounding cross. "It was an accident."

Talking's meant to help everything, that's what my parents say, that's what Suravi said, and even I basically think that. But Maika was sounding cross about the fact that she broke my wrist. Unless she was cross about the fact that I didn't sound sorry? Anyway, talking hadn't helped at all so far.

We looked at each other for about three seconds. Maika still looked sad, and I'm pretty sure I looked unhappy as well. I wanted to fix the problem between us, and I thought she did too, but we didn't seem to know how. Our feet suddenly got wet because the sea had breached the wall. We started digging, desperately shoring up the undermined wall, knocking down the turret to repair the hole. The sea ringed us and flowery Barbie entirely, cutting us off from dry land.

I stopped digging and stood up, wishing I could think of something helpful or thoughtful to say to Maika. Because I used to go to her birthday parties, and play on her PlayStation, and swing on the rope over the river with her. We ran away from an angry horse together. And because when I'd watched her singing in York, I'd felt a deep ache in my chest and a wave of sadness that I couldn't quite explain.

She stood up too. Neither of us said anything for a bit, we just looked at the sea again.

"OK," she said finally. "There's stuff I haven't told anyone except my mum and my sister and Suravi." She sighed a long sigh and looked at flowery Barbie, stuck in the top of our pile of sand. I wondered what was coming.

But before she could say anything else, Barney charged past us, holding two cones topped with three scoops of ice cream.

"I'm going to reason with it!" he yelled, and kept charging into the sea, so the water was lapping over his shoes and above his ankles. "Take me!" he cried, striding out towards the horizon. "Leave the others, it's me you want!"

The water continued to flood in, around Barney, through his legs, breaking against his shins. He stood there, poised somewhere between coming back and wading on out into the North Sea, until a larger wave approached, and he ran back, jumped over our ruined wall and joined us, handing me one of the cones. Suravi came in too, squeezing in next to us, giving Maika a cone. It was a very crowded sandcastle.

"We're going to get stranded!" Suravi said, laughing.

"We'll be adopted by dolphins," Barney said.

So we waited behind our crumbling wall for the sea to win, like the sea always wins. But something amazing happened. The last bits of the wall held. We kept mostly dry, apart from Barney. The sea jostled pointlessly around us for a while, and then began its long retreat. The Barbie-topped castle avoided becoming a glorious failure. It turned out to be indestructible instead.

Suravi picked a shell out of the walls.

"I'm going to keep this," she said. "If they kick me out

and I'm at some other school, I'll put this next to my ear and I'll hear Barney yelling at the tide."

"Wish I'd yelled something more interesting now," Barney said.

We stepped out of the remains of our castle. Maika picked up her battered Barbie and put it away, and we started pulling on our clothes over our damp costumes. It was getting cooler.

Suravi was looking at us suspiciously. "You two all right?" she said. "Talked about stuff?"

We both smiled at her and said, "Yes." She looked unconvinced, which was fair enough, because we were completely unconvincing. We had talked about stuff, a bit, but we still weren't all right. I had no idea what she'd been about to tell me when Barney showed up.

Barney was trying to squeeze the water out of his socks while he was still wearing them. He looked up. "I don't want to be the one to say it," he said, "but someone's got to. Is it time to go home?"

He looked at me. So did Maika and Suravi.

I took a deep breath.

This was the moment.

"OK," I said. "Here's the thing. I'm not actually going home."

FIFTEEN

There was a second of shocked silence before Barney and Suravi started yelling at me.

Suravi: "What are you talking about?"

Barney: "We're going back this afternoon!"

"I know," I said, holding my hands up. "I know, I know!"

Maika wasn't yelling. She just stared at me.

I shook my head. I sort of batted the air with my hands. I opened and closed my mouth. Now we'd finally arrived at this moment, I wasn't sure what to say.

Maika put her palm flat on my chest, like she wanted to feel my heartbeat. She looked right into my eyes. "Stop waving your hands and gawping. Take a deep breath. Then, when you're ready, tell us what's going on."

I sighed, stuffed my hands in my pockets, and took a breath. "OK, all right, fine," I said, and I kicked the sand and tutted, looking at my feet.

"So I've got this whole other thing that I want to do," I told them. "That I *need* to do. Scarborough was only ever going to be—"

"Phase One!" Suravi interrupted. "That's what you said when we got here."

I nodded. "My mum and dad want me to go to school and pretend like everything's normal," I mumbled. And then my hands were out of my pockets, waving in the air again, and I was suddenly loud, as if I was in the middle of an argument: "But it's not normal, is it?" Maybe I *was* in the middle of an argument, in my own head. "So I want to go and see Uncle Universe!" I blurted. "That's his nickname, because his brain's as big as the universe, and he's a doctor and he promised he'd help me, so why shouldn't I?"

It had all been going round and round in my head since Friday on the shed roof when I'd first thought of it. So, OK, it came out a bit jumbled, but it mostly made sense to me. It was my plan. My mostly sane plan.

But they were all still looking at me, like they didn't understand at all.

"Why did you lie about it?" Barney said.

"Where even is Uncle Universe?" said Suravi.

Maika was just staring again.

Before I could answer, I got a text from my mum, checking we were getting the 4:07 train. Suravi's phone buzzed too. We didn't answer.

"I lied because it wasn't fair to drag you along with me. And he lives just up the coast" – I pointed – "in Robin Hood's Bay."

A toddler ran screaming past us with a ball in her arms, and her mum chased her, swerving round me, shouting, "Sorry!" I felt weird talking about this on the beach, surrounded by people, with the tide coming in.

"Can we please go back to the flat, please?" I said.

We walked up the steep hill towards the castle. They nagged me to keep explaining, but I refused, partly because the hill was too steep to talk and climb, and partly because I needed this short walk to calm down and think about what I was going to say. I kept half an eye out for our creepy neighbour, though. *What had he been doing? Why was he looking through our stuff?* "Creepy" didn't seem to cut it any more.

Maika let us into our house. Up all the stairs, and then finally we were in the flat. We dumped our bags, and everyone looked at me.

"Could do with a shower," I said.

"Shut up," said Suravi. "Sit down. We still don't know what you're talking about."

"Your mum and dad want everything to be normal, and everything's not normal, we get that," said Barney. "But I'm sorry, I didn't understand literally anything else that you said."

Suravi nodded. "Who's Uncle Universe?"

145

"Uncle Universe is my uncle," I told them. "He's Uncle Harvey, my mum's brother, and he lives in Robin Hood's Bay, like I said, which is just down the road." I gestured again, as if we could look out of the window and see it. I was talking slowly now, and not shouting any more, trying to explain it "clearly and step-by-step", the way Mr Locke likes it. I wanted them to understand.

"Him and my mum, about nine years ago, they had this huge argument. It was something about money, my grandma's will, I don't know. But he wrote me a letter which said that he might not see me for a while, and he promised that if I ever needed him, he'd be there for me." I stared at them all, wanting to be sure they understood. "Robin Hood's Bay is, like, ten miles away. I'll get a bus there, or a taxi, but I need to see Uncle Universe, that's all."

They all stared back at me. They still didn't look like they understood at all. Suravi lifted a finger. "Thing is, Jasper," she said slowly, "I don't know if this makes sense." Her voice was all soft and quiet now, not like her normal voice at all. "What can your uncle say or do that will make a difference?"

I knew this would happen. I knew that as soon as my plan got exposed to other people, they'd start pulling it apart. I made a real effort to make my voice sound calm and reasonable. "I have to see him and talk to him," I said, "because he's brilliant. I don't mean he's brilliant like he's great, like he's a nice guy. I mean he's actually brilliant.

His own parents said he had a brain as big as the universe, which is how he got his nickname. And he promised he'd help me. Anything I need, that's what he said in his letter, absolutely anything, he even underlined it. My parents didn't say that; the doctor didn't say that. Only he said that."

They stared at me.

Barney bit his lip.

Suravi and Maika exchanged a glance.

"OK, he promised he'd help you," Suravi said. "But I still don't get what he can actually ... do."

I swallowed. This would have been a good moment to tell her exactly what he could do, to tick off a few practical, detailed ways he could make a difference. But I didn't have any detail. I just believed in Uncle Universe. He was a massive-brained doctor, possibly even a cancer doctor, who told amazing stories, and I was pretty sure there was no danger of him telling me to **CARRY ON AS NORMAL!** I thought I'd have a better chance of avoiding Option Three with him; and I thought if I lived with him I'd be happier, I'd have some control over my life. So even if he wasn't actually magic like he'd told six-year-old me, he basically had magical qualities.

I couldn't pretend it was logical, but it made sense to me. "I feel like I have to do this." I sighed.

Suravi was frowning, Barney's mouth was open, Maika was pursing her lips. My chest was tight and I felt short of breath. I took a gulp of air and let it out slowly. "So anyway," I said, "the point is: it's fine." I was nodding at them, waiting for them to agree. "We've had a great time and I'm really glad you came with me, but now you should go home, because otherwise you'll get into massive trouble. I was always going to do this next bit on my own. Phase Two. So you can all go, because it's fine – I'll be fine." More nodding. "Seriously, I'll be fine."

I might have carried on talking, I might have said "fine" a couple more times, but then Maika spoke up.

"I get it," she said.

Maika said that! It was down to her we were in this great flat in Scarborough, and now she was on my side at this crucial moment!

"Sometimes there's things that you just need to do," she continued. "They don't have to make sense, but if you don't do them then you feel … out of control."

We all stared at her. Suravi put a hand on her arm but Maika didn't look at Suravi, she was looking at me. I nodded again, slowly this time. "Yeah," I told her, "you're right – it's a thing I need to do. But also, it does make sense, because he promised he could help me, and I've got it in writing."

I waved my hand vaguely towards the door. "So you guys, you should … you know… You should go home now, because—"

Suravi lifted her finger again. "Stop talking," she said.

Really, *her* calling *me* bossy was about the most ridiculous thing that had ever happened. She and Maika and Barney all huddled up and started whispering, voices quiet but intense. What were they whispering about? Probably what they were going to tell their parents. And my parents, in fact, when they got home without me.

They all turned round. "Yeah," Suravi said. "We're coming with you."

I stared at her. Then I shook my head so hard it made my eyes itch. "No," I said. "No, no, no. You can't do that. This isn't your problem, it's my problem."

"Yes," Suravi nodded, "it is your problem, but we're your friends, and we're not going to just leave you here."

"But still—" I began.

"Also," Suravi interrupted, "maybe we don't want to fully run away, but none of us want to go back to school right now either." She pointed first at Barney, then Maika, then herself. "He's getting a hard time from Joe Hancock, she gets anxious, I'm right on the edge of getting chucked out."

"But you didn't throw that chair at Miss Alam!" I said. "You didn't even throw it at that girl who called you 'Subaru'. You just threw it away. Me and Barney saw the whole thing! We'll tell Miss Alam."

Suravi shook her head like I was completely missing the point. "The thing is," she said, "none of us want to be at school. At all. So we'll take a few days off and we'll do this together."

149

I thought of us all on the shed roof in my garden after school on Friday; all of them agreeing to running away without an argument, as if the idea had been floating around in their heads already.

"OK," I said, "but still—"

"We've decided!" It was Barney interrupting this time. "End of."

I looked at him. "Joe Hancock?"

He looked at the floor. "He's always on my case."

"I'm sorry, I didn't know."

He shrugged. "You've been busy."

I turned to Maika. She looked defensive, like she was ready for me to say something mean. "I honestly am sorry I called you a nutter," I told her. "You're not a nutter."

She did a small nod.

She and I were definitely better than we'd been, but we weren't mates. Because I still didn't get it. I used one bad word; she made my life miserable for months *and* broke my wrist. Our eyes met for a couple of seconds, then flicked apart.

Still, I couldn't quite believe it. All of them supporting me – even Maika.

"Thank you," I said. It came out as a whisper.

So this was mostly a good moment, but it was a long way off perfect. Because Barney was being bullied, Suravi might get chucked out of school, and Maika and I still weren't right. And she was anxious. And, most of all, because I was still lying to them. I hadn't told them yet that I was planning to move in with Uncle Universe, not just visit him, so that I could make a fresh start, give myself the best chance of avoiding Option Three and incidentally show the world that I didn't want to be treated like a kid.

So my *new* plan was that we'd all go to Robin Hood's Bay together, they'd stay a night or two, then they'd leave. And I wouldn't.

"OK!" Suravi clapped her hands. "So that's all sorted. Nice. Now let's see how much money we've got."

We put all our notes and coins on the table.

ME:	£4.66
SURAVI:	£12.45
MAIKA:	£18.17
BARNEY:	£9.92
BUSKING:	£14.62
TOTAL:	**£59.82**

"Blimey," I said. "That'll do."

Maika smiled. "Fifty-nine pounds and eighty-two pence."

Barney laughed. "Fifty-nine actual pounds and eighty-two pence! I've never seen that much dosh all at once."

We added our debit cards to the pile of cash and Suravi tapped hers. "I've got nearly a hundred quid in my bank account from babysitting and stuff. We're officially rolling in it. We can share a cab to your uncle's, you can talk to him tonight, and then tomorrow probably, or Tuesday, we all go home. Right?"

I didn't answer that. "Can I have that shower now?" I asked. "Then we better agree what we're telling our parents."

Milo was scratching at the door. "I'll take him out," Barney said.

He and Milo went out, Suravi and Maika went in their room to pack, I got in the shower. "*It is your problem, but we're your friends.*" That was about the nicest thing that anyone outside my family had ever said to me. "*We're not going to just leave you here.*"

I tipped my face up into the stream of warm water. I felt pretty good. I had another day or two with Suravi, Barney and Maika, so I was happy about that. I shook my head, soaped myself all over. Sand swirled down the plughole.

Not everything was perfect. I was worried about my friends, and things with Maika were still a bit weird. "*She gets anxious.*" What exactly did that mean? And I was still worried that Uncle Universe might not even be at the address I had, or might not want to see me. But I felt good anyway, mostly, because Phase Two of running away was about to start: the bit of the plan that involved finding Uncle Universe. And it turned out I wasn't going to be alone.

I washed all the soap off, stepped out of the shower,

and came out of the bathroom with a towel wrapped round me. Barney had left the flat door open. That was a bit careless. I looked at the table. The table where all our money had been. Fifty-nine pounds and eighty-two pence. Plus our bank cards.

There was nothing there.

SIXTEEN

"It's gone!" I hammered on Suravi and Maika's bedroom door. "It's gone!"

Maika opened up. "What's gone?"

"All our money! It's not on the table. Have you got it? Did you move it?"

The shock in her face was all the answer I needed. Suravi pushed past her. "It can't have gone."

We all went back out to the sitting room. "I mean, look," I said, pointing at the table, my voice quivering. "Pretty sure it's not there!"

"All right, calm down, Drama Queen," Suravi said. "Barney … maybe Barney's got it."

I looked at the open door. "No," I said. "Why would he?" I shook my head, suddenly understanding. "I know who's got it." I raced out into the passage with Suravi and Maika behind me and hammered on our neighbour's door.

He opened up, smiling smugly. It was the first time I'd seen him smiling and I was pretty sure I knew why.

"You! You stole our money!" I shouted, right in his face.

He looked puzzled. Or at least, he looked like someone doing a silly puzzled face – forehead wrinkled, lips pushed out, head tilted.

"Right," he said in his mean, nasal voice that sounded like a splinter in your thumb. "That's a serious accusation, isn't it?"

"You were trying to steal our stuff on the beach, and now you've come into our flat and stolen our cash!" My finger jabbed towards the window, then back to our place as I spoke. "And you don't even know or care but I really, really need that money!" My voice was doing that annoying, squeaky, quivering thing again.

"Hmm," he hummed, all calm, as if he was giving this some serious thought. "Interesting. What do you need it for?"

I opened my mouth. Closed it.

His smile got bigger, as if he'd guessed right about something. "You're all obviously up to no good," he said. "Tell you what, we better call the police. Don't you think?"

Barney came back with Milo, who barked when he saw our neighbour. "What's going on?" he asked.

Flat Face looked at Barney, glanced at the dog, and finally looked back at me. "Nothing," he said. "Nothing

155

at all is going on." He smiled at me again. "Right, son?" And then he shut the door in my face.

We went back in the flat and sat around the empty table where all our money had been. We got on our phones and cancelled our bank cards.

"We should definitely call the cops," said Barney. "Except we can't, because they'll talk to our parents."

"We've still got our return tickets," said Maika slowly, as if it was hard to get the words out. "Should we just … go back?"

Suravi looked at me. "I think we have to," she said. "Don't we?"

I couldn't meet Suravi's eyes. I couldn't look at any of them. I put my face in my hands. I needed to think. I needed to think, but I couldn't think. I used to have a hoodie that said "Doomy Doomy Doom" on it. It was a joke present from my parents because I'm optimistic – I usually look on the bright side of every situation. But now it felt about right. It felt like doomy bad luck was hanging over me. And if that was the case, then I was probably heading straight for Option Three because that was the worst luck of all.

"What you thinking?" Barney asked, quietly.

"I'm thinking bad luck's hanging over me," I said through my fingers, and then I lowered my hands and looked at my friends.

"You should all go home," I said. "Definitely. But I'm staying. I'm going to walk to Uncle Universe's house. I'm just going to walk there. I have to."

"No way!" Barney squeaked.

"You can't!" Suravi slapped her hand on the table.

"Really bad idea," said Maika, shaking her head.

I ignored them all. The map I'd found at breakfast time was lying on the floor, half unfolded. I went and got it, finished unfolding it, laid it on the table and pretended I was studying it. I wasn't really, though. I mean my eyes were on it, but it didn't make any sense. It was just loads and loads of lines, mostly in small, squashed, wonky squares like a maths problem in Mr Locke's class, and big patches of green and yellow, and funny words like "Hawsker" and "Sneaton". But I was keeping my eyes on it so I didn't have to look at my friends. This was difficult for them, but it was definitely time for them to go. Mainly because we had no money.

Suravi sighed.

Barney chewed the inside of his cheek. "We could all come back and find Uncle Universe another time?" he said.

I shook my head. "I'm here now," I told him. I tried to sound upbeat. "And I'll be OK. It's just a short walk, and I've got a map!"

Suravi looked at Maika. They both looked at Barney.

"What?" I said.

Barney nodded. Maika nodded too.

"Yeah," said Suravi. "We're coming with you. All right, we've got no money, but we're still your friends, and we're still not going to just leave you here."

I stared at them. "*Nooo*," I said, drawing it out, shaking my head.

Suravi lifted a finger. "Don't even," she told me.

"We're coming!" Barney shouted.

Maika just nodded again.

I stared at them for a while, without saying anything, but I could basically see straight away that there was no point in trying to argue. So I didn't.

I did something much, much worse.

"Thanks," I said. "OK, unbelievable. Thanks."

I stuffed the map I couldn't read in my bag and started making peanut-butter sandwiches, like I was confident and I knew what I was doing. I put a bottle of water in my bag to go along with the letter, T-shirt, underpants and wet swimming costume.

Because I was being all calm and efficient, they all went off to pack. The moment they'd gone I took out my phone and wrote a text.

> Staying another night. Everything's fine. Lots of love. xx

My finger hovered over the send arrow. I had a feeling that what I was about to do was selfish and wrong. I mean, it was more than a feeling – it was definitely selfish and wrong. But somehow it made no difference. I knew it wasn't completely rational, and on top of that I was quite scared, but it didn't matter. My parents didn't get it. I couldn't **CARRY ON AS NORMAL!** because nothing was normal, it just wasn't, and it didn't make sense to pretend that it was. Steve had entered my life. He was just visiting, I hoped, but he'd shoved everything else aside and made himself comfortable, and it was impossible to pretend he wasn't there.

If I stayed with Uncle Universe for a while my life would change. And change was what I needed.

I tapped the send arrow, turned off the phone, then left it on the table. I didn't want my parents ringing me or using the phone to track my movements. I could hear Suravi and Maika talking. They sounded excited and nervous. Milo barked. I felt a big bubble of regret in my chest about abandoning my friends, but I squashed it down and slipped quietly out of the flat. I left the door ajar so as not to make a noise, and then I ran down the stairs and out of the front door.

And I kept running. I went straight out on to the road overlooking the bay where I'd been that morning, which felt like about a hundred years ago, and I jogged as fast as I could down the hill towards Peasholm Park and the Sea Life Centre. Because it wasn't fair to involve Suravi and Barney and Maika. I didn't believe they'd ever really wanted to run away. They'd wanted a break from their lives and they'd wanted to support me, and I appreciated that, but they were already going to be in big trouble with their parents. I didn't want to make things any worse for them.

Phase Two of running away had begun.

And I was going to find Uncle Universe.

SEVENTEEN

So there I was, running along the ragged edge of England, puffing and panting, heading for the Cleveland Way. And there were Suravi, Barney and Maika, still in the flat, just realizing that I'd disappeared.

At this point, I need to tell you about stuff that wasn't happening to me but which I heard about later, because it's relevant.

First of all, Suravi completely lost it, obviously. Apparently, she was yelling at me even though I wasn't there and she was yelling at Maika and Barney too, even though it wasn't their fault. I bet she felt like throwing a chair. They all ran out into the street but there was no sign of me. I had the map and they had no clue which direction Robin Hood's Bay was.

Suravi was still stamping around and shouting, and Maika had to tell her to calm down because Barney was getting really upset. Suravi apologized and then they all took a big deep breath and tried to decide what to do.

Barney got his phone out and started checking the route to Robin Hood's Bay. He was holding the screen up close to his face, but Suravi put a hand on his wrist and lowered it.

"What are you doing?" he snapped.

"If he doesn't want us to follow him…" She paused, shook her head slowly, then finally continued. "Maybe we shouldn't follow him."

Barney stared at her.

"He's made a choice," Maika said quietly. "We should probably respect it. He's going to see his uncle. Turns out, that's what this was all about."

They trudged back up to the flat in silence, probably because they realized that this trip wasn't about them. I think they felt like they were basically irrelevant.

So they finally decided to go home.

Meanwhile, I was jogging – or just fast-walking – past a long line of hotels and B&Bs all squashed together, all looking out to the sea. I went steadily downhill, and when I got to the park I turned right at the crazy golf on the corner and walked out on to the beach. I felt rubbish about leaving my friends, but the truth is I also felt good about finally setting off on Phase Two of my journey.

"Nothing to worry about!" I said out loud.

A gull swooped down near my head, squealing, so close that I saw its claws and its fierce little eyes. I flinched and ducked as if it was attacking me, dive-bombing me, my hands raised protectively over my head. And then I felt like a fool. It wasn't attacking me. Seagulls don't attack people, not unless they're holding a sandwich. And do seagulls even have claws? (I was pretty sure that this one did.)

I passed a café, and I really wanted a hot drink but I literally didn't have a penny thanks to our creepy, flat-faced neighbour. Why was he like that? I wished people weren't so horrible. People like him and Joe Hancock and whoever sacked my dad. And that seagull, although the seagull didn't really count.

I realized I'd started walking a lot later than I should have, so it would be dark before long. I was on a broad concrete path, with seaweed-y rocks on my right and scrubby grass on my left, but the path would end soon, and you probably needed a compass and a geography A level to walk along the Cleveland Way. I didn't have either of those things. It felt weird not having my phone. About the only useful things I had were a map I couldn't read, and two peanut-butter sandwiches.

"Nothing to worry about," I muttered, less confidently.

At this point, Suravi, Barney and Maika were all walking back to the station. They were going pretty slowly, bickering a bit. They'd sent texts to their parents saying they were on the way home and they didn't know where I'd gone, and then they'd turned off their phones to avoid being hassled. Milo was trotting along beside them, looking up at Barney and whimpering because he could tell something was wrong.

At least they weren't yelling any more. They were really cross with me, though, and really worried, *and* wondering if they should have tried to follow me. Milo suddenly pulled on his lead and squatted on the pavement. Barney asked the girls to wait and led him off down a little side street.

Barney and Milo went a little way down the street, then Barney took off his rucksack and peered inside to look for a poo bag.

That's when it happened.

A guy with a baseball cap pulled low over his face strode up to Barney, scooped up Milo and sprinted away.

EIGHTEEN

I walked round the Sea Life Centre and along a last bit of promenade. There was a pub with tables and benches outside it – The Old Scalby Mill. I sat down, opened the map I couldn't read and looked hard at it. I couldn't even find Scarborough. What kind of a map was this? Maybe it really was only for proper explorers, and since I definitely wasn't a proper explorer, it was no help to me. No help at all. But surely I should be able to find Scarborough? It's not some little village. I ran my finger along the coastline. What was going on? Why did Scarborough not exist?

I was starting to panic when I tried turning the map over.

It was double-sided. There was Scarborough, next to the sea, right where it should be. There was gribbly pink stuff between the coast and the sea. I didn't know what that was: rocks maybe? But there was also a green line on the coast itself. That was the Cleveland Way. I followed it with my finger, turned the map over again and followed it some more. It went all the way to Robin Hood's Bay.

"Nothing to worry about." I forced the words out in a breathy little whisper. This was a bit scary, but as my mum always says about scary things, they make you larger. Not literally, though, so that was fine.

But how did I get on to the Cleveland Way?

As far as I could tell (and I knew I could be completely wrong) it was just sort of … there … really close to where I was sitting. I looked up. There was a footbridge across a little stream and there were some steps beyond it cut into the hillside. There was a sign. Maybe the sign said *The Cleveland Way*.

A couple of people went into the pub. I was tempted to follow them. My scared feeling was growing, my confidence was shrinking, and I knew I shouldn't be here. It was obviously wrong that I was sitting here, on my own, on the edge of Scarborough, while it was starting to get dark. I could just go in the pub, beg to use a phone and call my mum. It felt like my last chance. My whole body was sort of stretching towards the pub. I could forget about searching for Uncle Universe and moving in with him. I could give up on the whole plan, which had always felt sort of sane at the centre and ridiculous at the edges.

I sat there, trying to decide what to do.

Then I folded up the map, which took several attempts.

I stood up. And then I paused there another minute, one more minute, looking at the solid white walls of the pub. My feet were sort of shuffling like they couldn't make their minds up.

I didn't want to whisper *Nothing to worry about* any more, because there were a couple of things to worry about. So, instead, I made a list of the worrying things in my head.

1. Getting lost
2. Falling into a ditch, breaking my ankle or my wrist again, and starving to death or dying of cold
3. Getting kidnapped
4. Getting attacked by wild animals:
   a. Seagulls with claws
   b. Wolves

It helped, actually. Because once the worrying things were there in a list, I decided that number one was quite possible but not the end of the world, and numbers two, three and especially four were pretty unlikely. So I didn't whisper *Nothing to worry about*, I whispered, "Come on!" instead.

Finally, I set off across the footbridge.

It turned out the sign didn't say *The Cleveland Way*. It said:

BEWARE: DANGEROUS CLIFFS

Well, that was a new one. I mean, I'd add it to my list of things to worry about, but it wasn't going at the top. How dangerous could cliffs be? Just don't fall off them. I felt like the sign should say, "BEWARE: SCARY PATH THROUGH THE WILDERNESS." That would be more accurate. "YOU MIGHT LOSE YOUR WAY." But, you know, you'd probably find it again. "THERE MIGHT BE WOLVES." But there probably wouldn't be.

I kept going, up the steps cut into the hillside. I wasn't beware-ing at all, I was doing the opposite. Up the steps and on to the top of the hill, which wasn't actually a hill because it was a "DANGEROUS CLIFF" ... apparently.

The path ahead was clear and obvious. It was a narrow dirt path fringed by grass, with the edge of the cliff on one side and fields on the other. It was the Cleveland Way. Had to be.

Right. Robin Hood's Bay, here I come!

I walked for ages, first quickly, then more steadily, then quite slowly. My trainers scuff-scuffing on the path, my rucksack getting heavier on my back, rubbing against my sore shoulder, my legs starting to feel tired. The cool breeze in my face. I was trying not to think proper thoughts, just concentrating on where I put my feet and looking at the view.

I wanted to eat up the miles and get there in record

time, but also I didn't want to wear myself out too quickly, so I stopped and checked my watch to see how long I'd been going. (I'm the only person my age I know who wears a watch, and mine has a stretchy gold strap because it used to belong to my granddad who I was named after.) I stared at it. I thought my granddad's useless watch had stopped, it must have stopped, but the second hand was tick-tick-ticking round the face.

Apparently, I hadn't been walking for *ages*. I'd only been going for eleven minutes.

I sighed. OK, maybe I should try walking in eleven-minute bursts. I got going again, same as before, quickly at first, then steadily, then really quite slowly. Trainers scuff-scuffing, breeze on my face, no thoughts, watching my feet, looking at the view. My back was getting sweaty and I felt like I might be getting a blister. There were tall spiky bushes on one side of the path now, and long yellow grass on the other, and the light was going grey because the sun was going down.

I stopped again. Checked my watch. I'd only done eight minutes this time.

There was a smell of dry earth and manure, and something was rustling in the spiky bushes. The good news was, it sounded like it was pretty small, so it probably wasn't a wolf. The bad news was, there was no way I was going to reach Robin Hood's Bay before it got dark. It was about ten miles away (if I didn't get lost), which was going to take a lot of eleven- and eight-minute bursts. I started walking again, not quickly this time, just trying to keep up a slow, steady pace. Despite my best efforts, thoughts kept barging in where they weren't wanted. Thoughts about my parents being angry and worried, and my friends also being angry and worried. *Had I done the right thing, leaving them behind?*

My shoulder was aching, so I was also thinking about Option Three because I was basically *always* thinking about Option Three. It was still squatting inside my head like a black toad. This whole trip was supposed to take my mind off it, which had worked fairly well, but now I was on my own and there it was again: ugly and croaking and wrong, making me feel sad and scared.

And soon I was going to be walking in the dark.

After what felt like a long time (I decided not to check my watch), I came to a bench overlooking another bay. So I stopped and sat down. It was nice to find a bench because it meant people walked along here sometimes, so it couldn't be that isolated. There probably weren't wolves. It was also nice because my legs were really tired and I thought I probably did have a blister on my foot. The cliff edge was in front of me and I could see a pebbly beach right down there at the bottom, and then the sea. Behind me there was a steep slope down to a valley with trees in it. It was properly getting dark now and it was starting to spit with rain too. And my shoulder was still aching.

"Right," I muttered out loud. "Now what?"

I was on my own in the middle of nowhere with an achy shoulder and cancer. And a blister. And I was starting to wonder why I'd left Suravi, Barney and Maika in Scarborough. They'd wanted to come with me! "*It is your problem, but we're your friends.*"

A small part of me wanted to turn back. This was probably my last chance to turn round and head back to that pub with the white walls. It was about half an hour's walk away. I'd get there before it was really seriously dark – I'd call my parents. And I'd give up.

I thought of the Jasper in Uncle Universe's story finding himself in a world where nothing was right, where nothing made sense any more. Suddenly hanging in the sky with a rowing boat coming towards him. That was me. When Steve arrived in my life I was suddenly hanging in the sky, and a rowing boat was coming towards me with only bad things inside it.

So, what was I doing now? Sitting here, on this bench, stuck somewhere between "I don't know" and "Who cares?" Was this actually helping? I was confused, because I'd never had a visit from Steve before, and I didn't know what to do. Running away and moving in with Uncle Universe had felt right when I was on the shed roof at home, and it had mostly felt right when I was on the beach in Scarborough, but there was a chance, a decent chance, that actually it wasn't right at all. Maybe it was just an irrational plan – as irrational as running away to Las Vegas or New York.

Here I was. Bench. Middle of nowhere. Tempted to turn back. But I needed to find Uncle Universe, that was the thing to hang on to. He was a doctor, and he was brilliant, and it had always felt like he was a little bit magic, like Dr Who or Dr Strange, and he'd promised to help me. And I definitely needed help. So I couldn't turn back. I just couldn't.

I murmured it again. "Now what?"

And, unexpectedly, I got an answer. There was a sudden sound behind me: a bark. I jumped. I turned slowly and saw a black Labrador sitting there, head tilted, staring at me.

"Oh," I said. "Hi."

Bit late for dog walking. I looked round for his owner, but there was no sign of anyone. I patted my leg and he came tentatively towards me. I scritched him behind the ears. "What's your name?" I asked. No answer. And he didn't have a collar.

The nameless dog wasn't helping. I dithered again, like I had outside the pub. I sat on the bench, scratching the dog, shuffling my feet. I wasn't going to turn back. I'd come this far. I had a letter in my bag and the letter had the promise in it. But I wasn't going to get to Robin Hood's Bay tonight, so I needed shelter.

Right. That was a decision.

"Shelter."

I said it quite loud, but my voice disappeared in all the endless space in front of me – the bay, the sea, the sky, the whole, round world.

The dog heard it, though. He backed off from me and barked again. He crouched with his front paws stretched out in front of him and then he ran off down the steep slope, into the valley.

I followed him.

Once I would have rolled down this hill, hooting with laughter, racing Barney or Suravi or Maika, bumping into them, the world spinning wildly. Now I was trudging down, biting my lip. I tried humming "Rain on Me" as I walked, but that didn't help at all, partly because it actually *was* raining on me, and partly because it just made me miss my friends even more than I was already missing them.

And where was I going? Following a dog into some dark valley to sleep under a tree? That didn't seem sensible. Was it possible to lose your grip on reality and not notice? Because I was starting to worry that that was happening. Maybe it was a side effect of Steve.

All these doubts were churning around in my head but I kept walking down the hill. The Labrador ran ahead of me, looked back over its shoulder, then ran on.

Trees. Great rippling brown trunks stretching upwards, twisty branches, a roof of leaves. There was an insect-y buzz, chirps, rustles in the undergrowth. It got darker under the cover of all that greenery, but it also got drier. My watch said it was nearly seven o'clock but it felt later. I was thinking about my peanut-butter sandwiches now. I'd find a shallow hole; I'd put on an extra T-shirt and cover myself with leaves. Then I'd eat my sandwiches, possibly share them with the dog, and after that I'd see if I could get any sleep.

That was the plan.

But the plan changed pretty quickly, because at the bottom of the hill we arrived at a clearing. The Labrador came to a halt and turned to look at me, eyes big and expectant. I'd swear it was saying: *What do you think of this?* I swallowed nervously. Because what I saw was like something from a horror movie.

NINETEEN

THE CARAVAN IN THE WOODS – I could definitely imagine sitting in a dark cinema watching those words appear on the screen, dripping blood, with music like scraping fingernails coming out of the speakers.

It was in a clearing at the end of a scrubby, narrow track. A grimy grey box leaning over in a muddy puddle, as if it was in the middle of sinking. The light was fading, and the track led off into the trees, bending away, disappearing into murky green shadows.

My friendly Labrador had disappeared into the woods as if he'd done his job and that was that. Why had he disappeared? Was he scared of the caravan? Was there someone in there? Maybe it was the horror-movie guy that Suravi had imagined in York station. An axe murderer in a clown mask. I walked slowly all the way round it, keeping a safe distance, close to the trees. It had two filthy windows with ragged orange curtains drawn across them. One of its wheels had no tyre. No lights were on inside. It was grey in the grey light. It was like the ghost of a caravan.

It was abandoned. Probably. So it could be the ideal place to spend the night. Although the inside had most likely been used as a toilet ... and for drugs and sex and God knows what. Maybe some dog-scaring woodland animal lived in there, like a wolf. Definitely not an axe murderer, though. Probably not, anyway...

There was a shaft of dusty, pale evening sunshine that had found its way through the leaf cover, and I stood in the resulting pool of weak light, breathing in the wet green smell of moss. My fingers were pressed against a rough, ridged tree trunk. Rain was still spitting down on me.

What was I going to do?

I couldn't stand here all night.

OK, then. Time to try the door.

But I didn't move. I continued to just stand there, smelling the moss and rotting leaves, which probably smelled quite similar to dead bodies. It was very quiet. The only thing to hear was the patter of the rain, and I had a strange feeling. It started in my stomach and slid up, working its way into the folds of my brain. I was alone, somewhere dark, spooky and unfamiliar, I was cold and weary.

It felt possible that I was actually dead.

I might have quietly expired up on that bench, looking

out at the sea, and now I was a ghost. It genuinely felt like a thing that might have happened, and I found myself imagining dying in a way that I hadn't up to now. Not just a limb being amputated, but the rest of my life – sixty, seventy years – chopped off and gone.

I backed up against the tree I was standing next to and pressed my spine into it so hard that it hurt. I swallowed hard and looked down at my feet. I shuffled them backwards and forwards. And I still didn't move.

A ghost probably wouldn't be able to graze his back, he wouldn't be able to scuff up the earth.

I took a long slow breath and let it out in a quivering sigh.

A ghost wouldn't be able to breathe.

OK, then, I was pretty sure I was still alive.

"Come on," I whispered. "Come on, come on."

I was trying to encourage myself to move and also trying to drag myself out of my gloom. I stepped out of the pool of light, which already seemed darker. Hesitated, swallowed again, then stepped forward. Nothing to hear except the rain and a rustling of leaves. And my footsteps. I was trying to be quiet but I wasn't doing a great job of it, scrunching on leaves and twigs in a completely unghostly way. I crept, not quietly, up to the door of the caravan and put my hand on the handle.

A dog barked.

I mean, I say "a dog", and I say "barked" – this wasn't the Labrador politely drawing attention to itself, this sounded like a hell-demon, or, in fact, multiple hell-demons completely losing their minds. It was a sudden, ear-splitting eruption of noise. I fell backwards on to the ground, gasped, managed not to scream, and scrambled away on my bum. I got up on my feet, ran back to the nearest tree and hid behind it. The barking stopped.

I expected the door of the caravan to bang open and the serial killer in the clown mask to charge out waving his axe.

But no one came.

I stayed behind my tree because it could have been a trap. He could have been waiting for me to tiptoe out of hiding before he ambushed me. So I didn't move. I stayed where I was, and the dogs started barking again. Definitely dogs, not hell-demons. At least two. Maybe more. It was like the caravan was a radio and it was playing a soundtrack called "Dogs Going Wild". The sides were pretty much vibrating

And still no one came out.

I didn't know what to do.

There was obviously no one in there. If there was, they'd have come out by now to see who was disturbing their dogs. Maybe the owner of the dogs had died, and his half-eaten body was lying on the floor in there? I shivered. Axe murderers and half-eaten bodies – why did this sort of stuff come into my head? I really needed to get death off my mind.

"Come on," I muttered again.

I shook my head, as if to shake out the murderers and dead bodies.

"Come on, come on…"

I needed to separate things out sensibly. Were axe-murderers, wolves and half-eaten bodies scarier than Steve turning up and barging right into my body? No. No, they weren't. Well … yes, actually they were a bit, but they were also, unlike Steve, not real. I was coping with Steve, arguably. Possibly. OK, not really, but still, surely I could deal with a caravan with some dogs in it?

I took a couple of deep breaths, then came out from behind the tree and marched back towards the caravan. And the Labrador appeared and joined me. It seemed like we'd both decided to be brave.

"Good boy," I said lamely.

I could hear snuffling on the other side of the door, a whimper, but no barking. I laid my hand gently on the handle again. Had a good look around in the dusky light. Shadows and small dark shapes (bushes, not wolves), and looming, huge dark shapes (trees, not giants). The faint smell of the sea.

I looked back at the door and slowly, carefully, turned the handle and opened it a crack.

I left the Labrador sitting outside, and I squeezed into the caravan.

Dogs.

Not two dogs, more dogs. Basically, nothing but dogs.

Dogs on the floor, dogs on the seats, dogs on the table. All the dogs. An enormous great husky and a little poodle and another Labrador and a spaniel and breeds I couldn't name, all barking and yapping and full-on howling. I put my hands over my ears, but I also needed a third hand to put over my nose. The caravan stank of poo and piss and just general dogginess, and there was fur everywhere, tongues hanging out, mouths drooling saliva, teeth, and big, needy, liquid eyes and dogs, dogs, dogs.

And Milo.

Wait.

Milo?

It really was all the dogs.

All the dogs, including Milo.

"Milo?" He was scampering towards me, pushing past a collie and a spaniel, and I wasn't sure if he could hear me over all the barking.

"Milo, is that you?"

He squeezed between the other two dogs and jumped up, his paws on my knees, panting and barking. Milo wore a green collar and this dog didn't have one, but he was rusty red and shaggy and he was pointing his nose at me and lifting his little head like he was thinking about asking me a question, and he definitely seemed to know me.

"What are you doing here?" I asked him.

No answer. Duh.

I picked him up and hugged him anyway. I was sure it

was Milo. Seeing him, smelling him, having him lick my face, made me realize how lonely I'd been feeling. The table, which had a beagle standing on it, had a drawer in it. Still holding Milo, I opened it up. Nothing there. There were units along the side, with cupboards in them. I opened them up, found another drawer, opened that. Collars. Collars and leads. I sorted through them, chucking brown ones, red ones, black ones on the floor. Found a green one, checked it, chucked it away. Found another green one, checked it.

It was Milo's.

And underneath the collars there was a phone. It was a really rubbish phone, no way it had internet, but I grabbed it anyway, along with a lead.

OK, all right, I obviously couldn't sleep here, but I could get Milo out. He'd be company, which would be great because being on my own was definitely not fun, what with starting to think I was a ghost. First job, though: call Barney. Barney would be frantic.

I turned the phone on, praying it was charged enough. The screen lit up. Brilliant. But it was on 3%. Not so great. I called him, looking at Milo, putting a finger in my spare ear to try and block out dog noises, shifting my weight around restlessly.

It was ringing.

"Come on, come on, answer!"

He might see the call was from an unknown number and ignore it.

181

Still ringing. It went down to 2%.

"Come on, Barney, pick up."

I was gripping the phone hard, staring at Milo, who was staring at me.

"Hello?" His voice (Barney's, not Milo's) sounded miserable and suspicious.

"Barney, it's me, I've got Milo!"

"What? Jasper? What?" His voice wasn't miserable and suspicious any more, it was squeaky and shocked.

"Yes, Milo!" I told him where I was and what had happened, and I was about to ask him how he'd lost Milo and where he was, but I didn't have the chance.

I couldn't ask him anything because the caravan was suddenly flooded with intensely bright lights.

TWENTY

Headlights.

It wasn't a serial killer with an axe and a clown mask who owned this caravan, it was a dog thief. And I thought I could guess who it was.

"B-Barney," I stuttered, "Barney, I've got to—" The phone died.

I shoved it in my pocket and picked up Milo. He licked my face and sat happily in my arms like a big, hairy, face-licking baby.

"What are we going to do, Milo?"

He looked up at me, probably sensing my rising panic. He nuzzled my face and licked my cheek again. Friendly, but not helpful.

The headlights flicked off.

There was nowhere to hide in the caravan, it was just a small box full of dogs.

A car door slammed.

The dog thief was coming. He was walking towards the door right now.

The windows were much too small to climb out of. I darted my eyes around, head jerking from side to side. Caravans are clever, they have little cubby-holes and storage spaces; maybe if I'd had time I could have crawled into a cupboard or lifted up a seat and found space underneath it. But I didn't have time. I didn't have any time. So what was I going to do? Lie on the floor and cover myself in dogs? Milo whimpered.

They were all barking again. Even Milo, who was pressed up against my chest, started barking, and I couldn't think. I couldn't think! The dog thief was approaching, he was about to open the door, and I didn't know what to do.

I could barely breathe.

I kept hold of Milo, crooked in my left arm, and I scooped up a little pug with short, soft fur and deep wrinkles on his forehead. He looked up at me with enormous, dark, curious eyes as I held him in my shaking hand. "Sorry about this," I whispered. I heard a hand on the caravan door. The handle began to turn.

The door opened a crack and Flat Face, our creepy neighbour, peered in. He was holding the struggling, whimpering black Labrador in his arms.

He saw me and hesitated on the step, confused.

I saw him and hesitated too.

He opened his mouth to speak.

But before he could say a word in that mean, splintery voice of his, I kicked the door wide open and chucked the little pug right into his face.

He cried out, hands in the air, pug in his face, toppled out of the caravan and fell flat on his back on the ground. The pug and the Labrador yelped and ran off.

And then there was a dog explosion. Wait, that needs capitals, bigger letters, and an exclamation mark.

There was a **DOG EXPLOSION!**

Dogs burst out of the caravan door like a bomb going off and they stampeded over our creepy, flat-faced, dog-thief neighbour, barking, yelping and howling, trampling over every bit of him. It was a hairy, deafening, hundred-pawed waterfall of dogs, all tongues and claws and thwacking tails and doggy excitement, doggy panic and doggy joy, all streaming over his body. I joined them. I jumped on his stomach on purpose, heard him huff out a great gasp of air, and bounced off again. I kept going, running past his dirty red van and into the woods, sprinting, still clutching Milo, who was barking away, only pausing occasionally to lavishly lick my face, apparently having a great time.

"I'm dropping this one off on the way. Be with you in half an hour."

That's what he'd said in the street outside the flat. He was stashing stolen dogs here.

I ran.

I ran off the track and away from the caravan into the trees, in half-darkness, stumbling and nearly tripping loads of times over branches and roots and dogs. Especially dogs. I didn't know where I was going, I didn't know if Flat Face was following me, I was just running, my bag bouncing on my sweaty back, Milo bouncing in my arms, my shoulder hurting, my legs aching, my blister stinging. Milo was wriggling and whining and trying to escape now, wanting to do some running of his own. I didn't let him, I clung on tight and kept going, deeper into the trees.

I skidded to a stop at the foot of a huge oak, panting and exhausted, gasping in great, shaky breaths. I'm not very good at trees, but I was pretty sure it was an oak, judging by the curvy leaves in piles underneath it. Some of the roots were above ground, like fat, gnarly tentacles stretching out and digging into the earth. I sat down with a thud next to the largest of these roots, then I lay down beside it and wriggled underneath it and under the leaves. I was still holding Milo and now I held on to his snout too, keeping his jaws closed, trying to whisper breathless reassuring words into his floppy ear.

And then we just lay there. Me and Milo. In the dirt, under the leaves, under the root, at the foot of the tree. I could feel his heart beating fast and light against my chest, and I could hear my own heavy breathing, which was gradually slowing down.

So ... this was an odd place to be. Hiding under a pile

of leaves in the woods in the night-time, hunted by a flat-faced dog thief, somewhere off the Cleveland Way outside Scarborough. These woods were on his way somewhere; the caravan was a convenient place to stash dogs. Well, not any more. The truth is, I was pretty pleased with myself. I was the Dog Rescuer! And that buzzy feeling in my stomach – that was the opposite of carrying on as normal – was buzz-buzzing away. There were leaves tickling my nose, there was one insect crawling over the back of my hand, another creeping up my trouser leg, and there was a furious dog thief searching for me, but I didn't feel like a ghost at all.

In fact, Steve and Option Three felt almost irrelevant right now.

So maybe this was working out pretty well. My shoulder still throbbed and my legs were achy, I was cold and my foot was sore. There was still a chance I was going to get killed or at least beaten up. Milo might get stolen back. But the fact is, lying on the ground with Milo pressed against me, I was smiling.

His face when I threw the pug at him! He couldn't have looked more surprised if a number sixty-six bus had come out of the caravan door and run right over him.

Mind you, I'd forgotten to be hungry, but now I thought about it, I really was. It was probably time to eat my sandwiches. Soon. And I really missed my friends. I closed my eyes. Milo's chest was slowly rising and falling against mine. He was asleep. That was good. He'd had a pretty difficult time. I wondered what he'd been thinking, snatched from Barney, trapped in the caravan with all those other dogs.

Same as me, probably: *What on earth is going on in my life?*

I wasn't going to go to sleep, obviously – no chance of that – but I'd had a pretty difficult time too, one way and another. I could just lie here with my eyes closed for a while; I could just rest a while. Just rest…

A rustle of leaves. A twig cracking.

Milo was suddenly scrabbling his paws against my chest. He was about to bark but I clamped my hand round his snout.

"Shh," I told him.

I had no idea how long I'd been asleep.

Milo looked at me with bright excited eyes. I didn't think he knew. It was still dark, though. I mean, I was under a big pile of leaves, under a root, at the foot of a tree, but I could tell it was dark. I tried to keep Milo still, tried to huddle lower under the leaves, under the arching root. I was barely breathing because I could hear footsteps scrunching through leaves.

Was it him? Was it our creepy neighbour, carrying a big stick, or even an axe?

He was going to be cross. I mean, he was always cross, but I'd thrown a pug at his face, and released all the dogs he'd stolen in a **DOG EXPLOSION** and used his stomach as a trampoline, so it was safe to say he was going to be straight-up furious now.

A leaf was tickling my nose. I wanted to sneeze. *Don't sneeze*, I thought. Like that was going to help. The creature that had crept up my trouser leg was right up on my thigh now. I hoped it wasn't going to get into my pants and start biting or laying eggs.

And then Milo started wriggling frantically. He clawed at my chest, eyes wild. I tried to hold him, I really tried, but he pushed and wriggled and snapped, and snapped and wriggled and pushed, and suddenly he escaped from my grip and erupted from the leaves, barking wildly, and I followed him out, sitting up abruptly and hitting my head hard on the gnarly root above me.

I shouted "Ow!" and rubbed my head, my eyes closed.

Then I slowly, reluctantly, opened my eyes.

A dark figure was staring down at me.

TWENTY-ONE

It wasn't Flat Face.

It was Suravi.

And then Maika came up beside her. And Barney was behind her. He'd collapsed on to the ground with Milo in his arms. I stared at Suravi and Maika, blinking, rubbing my head.

"Hello, doughnut," Suravi said.

I rubbed my head some more, screwing up my eyes, squinting at them blearily, wondering if I was concussed or dreaming.

"But…" I said.

They waited.

"But what are you doing here?"

"Saving your life!" Suravi shouted. She really didn't need to shout; I was right in front of her.

"Again!" Maika was shouting too.

Barney sat up, holding Milo still on his lap. He didn't shout. He sounded sad and genuinely puzzled. "Why did you do it?" he said. "Why did you run off without us?"

And then they all stared at me.

I opened my mouth, and then I closed it again. I wasn't sure what to say.

"We're your friends, remember?" Suravi snapped. "In this together. Which bit of that do you not get?"

"I'm sorry," I mumbled.

"It felt like you just used us to get up here and find your uncle," Barney said.

"And once you were here, you ditched us," Suravi agreed.

"No!" I shook my head vigorously, which made it ache. "No, I wasn't using you. I wanted to spend this weekend with you, I really did, and I had a great time with you, all of you, but my plan was always to go on by myself. And then you were up for coming, but the money got stolen, so I thought it was too much to ask and ... and I didn't want you to get into trouble," I finished lamely.

Barney made a frustrated sound as he stood up. "We're OK with getting into trouble, you plank. We just want to help you. I thought you knew that."

"I do now," I said slowly. And then I apologized again because I wasn't sure what else to say. "I'm really sorry."

They all slowly swam into focus, all of them standing there, in the dark. They hadn't saved my life this time, that was a slight exaggeration, but still … it was such a surprise to see them; such a welcome, lovely surprise. They still looked cross with me and I didn't blame them, but I could feel that lump coming back into my throat because I was so happy and so relieved to see them and to not be alone any more.

"Thank you."

It was just two small words; my voice was small and it cracked a bit. It didn't feel like enough, but I didn't trust myself to say much more than that and I didn't know what else to say, so I stood up slowly and said it again.

"Thank you." And then I added, "Very much."

Suravi came in for a hug. "You fool," she whispered. Barney followed. Even Maika patted my shoulder. It was a nice, quiet moment, with dogs barking in the background and distant voices shouting.

"Thing is, though," said Barney, stepping away, "I told the police Milo had been stolen and then I also told them about your phone call, so if we don't want them to pick us up and take us all home we should get moving."

A torch beam was angling around a little way off, and far away (presumably by the caravan) a faint blue light started to flash. I was very happy that all the stolen dogs, including the black Labrador, were going to be found, that was definitely good news, but *I* didn't want to be found. I still wanted to get to Uncle Universe.

"All right," I said. "Shall we go?"

"We're not coming," said Suravi, as if that was obvious.

I stared at her. "Oh," I said. "Right…"

She cackled and pointed. "Your face! You are so gullible!"

We climbed back up the hill towards the coastal path, leaving the torches, the voices, the dogs and the blue light behind. I was stumbling in the dark again, stepping over roots, scrunching through leaves and occasionally ducking under branches. I felt exhausted and hungry, my blister hurt, my shoulder hurt, my legs were like two sacks of porridge, and Suravi was still laughing at me. But I was happy because I was with my friends.

Even though I had one last thing that I was holding back. One last thing to tell them. They weren't going to like it.

We stumbled through the trees, whispering, listening to dogs barking, spotting torchlight on the leaves. It felt unreal. I'd been sleeping, like, two minutes earlier, so I still wasn't completely sure that I wasn't dreaming. But I kept getting sharp, vivid flashes of Suravi's braid bouncing on her back, of Maika's blonde hair over her pink denim, of Barney giving me a grin. That helped. Also, whatever had been crawling up my thigh must have fallen out of my trouser leg, so that was more good news.

There was one worrying moment when I looked back over my shoulder and thought I saw something. A faint shadow in the darkness, disappearing suddenly as if it had moved behind a tree. But that was probably just my imagination. Like when I let scary thoughts of axe murderers and half-eaten bodies creep into my head. Steve's fault, probably. Except it wasn't really a *thought*, it was something I saw. Or *thought* I saw.

But I probably didn't see it, because it was dark after all, and I was still woozy.

I didn't say anything to my friends. I kept climbing the hill, kept my eyes on the uneven ground in front of me.

Finally, we staggered out of the trees, back on to the Cleveland Way. Half a moon was shining over the dark, restless sea and the sky was shimmering with a completely unrealistic number of stars – like roughly a billion. The narrow path stretched off along the clifftop. My little sleep had given me some energy, and Barney, Suravi and Maika all seemed to be fizzing with the excitement of having found me and found Milo, and Milo himself was jumping around like a puppy, and I remembered at that moment that I liked to think I was an optimistic person.

The nice thing, the really nice thing, was that it felt like we were all proper friends now. Me and Maika were still hesitant with each other, a bit wary, but she'd shown up. Here she was. Here they all were. So, whereas when we left home the problem was we all liked at least one other person in the group but none of us liked everyone, now basically everyone got on with everyone. You could see it in the way we were walking along the path: me and Suravi were basically walking backwards, so that we could talk to Maika and Barney as we went, although not completely backwards because we were walking along a cliff edge (*BEWARE!*). We were all feeling pretty good. I'd saved Milo, they'd saved me, and then forgiven me for being a fool. Creepy, flat-faced neighbour had probably been arrested – everything was going well.

But tiredness crept up on us. The porridge in my legs felt like it was filling me up: thick, sticky, grey porridge in my stomach and my chest and in my head. I'm not sure who yawned first but pretty soon we were all yawning, even Milo, and the energy we'd had after they'd found me all drained away.

"Look." Barney was pointing off the track, at a broken old bit of wall just barely visible in the distance. "Is that a... Is it a hut?"

No, it wasn't a hut. But it was more than just one bit of broken wall. It was a ruined old stone shed.

"Maybe a farmer used to sleep there," I said.

"Or maybe pigs did," said Maika.

"Let's check it out," said Suravi.

We trudged over a scrubby, muddy, uneven field towards the ruin. It wasn't raining any more, but the ground was still damp. Barney fell over and Milo barked at him.

"I'm fine," he said, getting up slowly.

"Did you fall in a cowpat?" Suravi asked, looking at him suspiciously.

"No," he told her, sniffing himself. "Don't think so."

There was a definite smell of poo in the air, but we all ignored it and kept going. An owl hooted as we reached the shed, stepped over a low bit of crumbled wall and went in. The remains of a fire were in a corner, and empty beer cans were lying around on the dirt floor. We looked at each other.

"We could find somewhere else?" Maika said.

Barney yawned. "I don't think I can walk another step."

"How are you less fit than me, when I've got Steve?" I asked him.

He smiled. "Yeah, but at least I don't walk out on my mates like my brain's actually stopped working," he said.

Suravi nodded. "Fair."

Barney sat down.

That decided it. We all sat down, and I got out the two peanut-butter sandwiches I'd made in the flat. I tore each of them in half and shared them out.

Suravi looked at her half a sandwich suspiciously. She sniffed it. "I don't like peanut butter," she said. "I don't like it so much that I feel sorry for people who do like it."

She still ate it, though. We all did, and we shared the bottle of water too. It wasn't much of a midnight feast. More of a midnight snack. It was like a very small starter to get you in the mood for a main course, but the main course never arrived. So we lay down. No one said much. We were too hungry and too tired to speak. We used our bags as pillows, we lay down on the damp earth under roughly a billion stars, and we closed our eyes.

The owl hooted again, as if to say goodnight.

Of course I couldn't sleep. Of course. The ground was hard and my legs were achy, my blister was still blistery. My stomach was demanding the main course that wasn't coming. My bag didn't make a good pillow, and there was definitely a smell of poo lingering in the air.

But none of that was the main problem. The main problem wasn't even the caravan that was parked in my head, or the dogs barking like hell-demons when I was about to open the door, or those headlights suddenly appearing, sweeping across the window, me trapped in that little box as someone walked towards it.

The main problem wasn't any of that, it was the fear of death that had ambushed me when I was standing in that pool of light. The sense that the whole rest of my life might just … not happen.

To get my mind off that, I started to make a mental list of all the things I'd done today. My shoulder was throbbing again and I rubbed it while I was thinking. Walking and eating, playing in the arcades, swimming and building a sandcastle, leaving my friends, rescuing dogs, being found by my friends. I clutched my shoulder and I thought – I didn't want to, but I did – I thought about trying to do those things with only one arm. I knew there were athletes who swam in races or skied with one arm, so I was pretty sure they'd be able to do all the things I'd done today. But still. I rubbed the little lump on my shoulder, stroked my hand all the way along my arm from my biceps down to my fingertips. Still.

I looked through the big hole in the roof up at the stars. I was back with my friends so I didn't have to feel lonely, but they were asleep and they didn't have cancer, they weren't lying awake worrying about Option Two and Option Three, so I did feel a bit lonely. It was that thing of being in a bubble, separated from even my very best friends, who weren't quite getting what I was feeling.

And tomorrow I was going to tell them that if I could find Uncle Universe, I was planning to stay up here with him. I couldn't put it off any longer.

Maybe it was because all the excitement was finally wearing off, but I felt small and sad. In the end, I did what I usually do when I can't sleep. I thought about Uncle Universe telling me the story of Jasper in Oswaldhover. And when I thought of him, and that story, I felt slightly better. I felt safer. Which just goes to prove, I thought, *Uncle Universe actually is a bit magic.*

Story-Jasper was in the rowing boat, in the sky, being kidnapped by an alien. They somehow left Earth and were pretty quickly somewhere else altogether. A different planet or a different dimension.

And what happened next? What did Jasper do in the story? He jumped.

MONDAY

TWENTY-TWO

I woke up with a lurch in my chest and a sharp breath, as if I really had just jumped. Eyes wide open.

It took me a minute to recover. The hard ground beneath me, my fingers scratching in dry earth. OK, I wasn't on a different planet or in a different dimension, I was in a field near Scarborough. My breathing slowed down.

That was a bit scary.

But I quite liked it too.

He jumped.

Till then, strange, frightening things had been happening to story-Jasper and he hadn't been able to do anything about them. He'd floated up into the air, he'd been abducted. But in this latest part of the story, it was different. He'd said, "No thanks, no more of that!" And he'd jumped right off the rowing boat. The only problem was, right now I couldn't remember what happened next.

So that was another reason to find Uncle Universe. He could tell me the end of the story.

I sat up, blinking sleepily, looking around in the grey, early-morning light. Life's simpler when you're at school. You always know what's happening next because your whole day is laid out for you. It was Monday morning, and I was supposed to be getting the bus to Rudding High soon, trying to **CARRY ON AS NORMAL!** Registration, then French, then computing and then … I couldn't even remember, but it was all there, a whole day, a whole term, waiting for me. I had a feeling hospital was going to be like that too, with sessions of chemo, doctors and nurses seeing me at particular times. Instead of that here I was: in a field, improvising, trying to find a way forward that made sense.

Everything ached. And I was really hungry. And oh, OK, now that I was properly awake there were lots of other problems, mostly around Uncle Universe and my parents. But I didn't want to think about my parents because it made me feel guilty, and I didn't want to think about Uncle Universe because it made me feel stressed.

So I stretched my spine instead, took a deep breath of cool morning air and I looked at my friends. Maika was on her side with her arms and legs stretched out like a broken ballet dancer, Barney was curled up like a hedgehog, Suravi was on her front like she'd fallen down dead. Her mouth was open and she was drooling a bit. They all looked like they'd been hovering twenty feet up in the air and then had dropped out of the sky. And I was pretty sure Barney had cow poo on his trousers.

I checked my granddad's watch. It was ten past six. No need to wake them yet.

Milo whimpered. He was probably hungry. Join the club. I stood up and did another stretch, a proper one this time with my arms and fingers straining outwards, and then I tipped my head back, looking up at the grey sky, doing a full-on hippo yawn. I didn't feel much better. I needed some breakfast, I needed to clean my teeth, and I needed about four more hours of sleep.

When I'd finished yawning, I saw that Maika was getting up.

"Morning," I whispered.

I thought I'd been pretty clever to bring sandwiches and a bottle of water and a map from the flat, but the really brilliant thing I'd done was bringing loo roll. I didn't even want to think about trying to use leaves. That would definitely not have gone well. I went off behind a bush, kicked earth over the mess, cleaned my hands on dewy grass, and then emerged and gave the roll to Maika.

After that, I went to look at the sea. I stood there on the clifftop with my hands behind my back, staring out like the King of Yorkshire. The sun was low and hazy over the water. It's big, the sea, and it changes colours even while you're looking at it. Plus it's got one of my top three favourite smells.

TOP SMELLS

1. Frying bacon (because obviously)
2. The sea (because it smells of holidays)
3. Cut grass (because it smells of summer)

Maika came and stood next to me, and we stared out at the sea together, not looking at each other.

"I really am sorry I broke your wrist," she said eventually. "I didn't mean to."

I nodded. She'd meant to trip me up on the stairs, that part was deliberate, but I knew she hadn't meant for me to fall down them and break an actual bone.

I glanced at her. She was looking at me now, and she was biting her lip.

"It's OK," I said.

I mean it wasn't, not entirely, but still.

"And I'm sorry you've got cancer," she said.

"Steve," I told her.

She tutted. "I can't say I'm sorry you've got Steve, that sounds silly."

She was right, it did. "All right, but you could say, 'I'm sorry *about* Steve'."

"Fine," she said impatiently. "I'm sorry *about* Steve!"

"You don't sound sorry."

I couldn't resist it. I repeated back to her what she'd said to me on the beach. The words just fell out of my mouth before I could stop them. It was meant to be more teasing than mean but it was definitely the wrong thing to say to her.

She sighed and stomped off back to the ruined shed, where Suravi and Barney were waking up.

So that didn't go very well. Me and Maika were still stepping carefully around each other, even now, even after she'd sort of saved my life twice. We were still trying to work out whether we liked each other any more, whether we could ever be proper friends again. There were moments when I thought we could, and then there were moments which revealed there was still something unspoken, something unexplored, stuck between us. I knew now that there was a story behind how she'd turned against me. Instead of pushing her away, I needed to find out what that story was.

I also knew that when I annoyed her, I felt bad about it. I missed her smile.

Barney and Suravi stood up, did the same sort of stretching and yawning I'd done, then each disappeared into the bushes in different directions, one after the other, with the loo roll.

And then at last we were ready to go. They all came trudging across the field towards me.

"I'm starving," said Barney, predictably. "And so is Milo."

"Maybe Milo could catch us a rabbit," Suravi said. "And we could skin it and cook it and have rabbit stew."

"Or you could get one with your Ninja throwing star," I suggested.

"Mm, rabbit stew," Barney said. "With roast potatoes and peas, and maybe with bacon mixed up in it."

"Milo can't catch a pig and vegetables," Suravi said.

"And hot apple and blackberry crumble with custard," Barney continued.

"Stop talking about food!" Maika snapped.

"Ice cream is way better than custard," I said.

"OK, but you're wrong," Barney told me.

We were walking along the path again, and it was actually quite nice at this point. Green fields as far as you could see on the left; blue, green and brown sea as far as you could see on the right. The problem was, the path stretched out ahead of us as far as we could see as well. We had some energy because we'd all slept a bit. But on the other hand, we were all starving.

"At least we're not at school," I said to take our minds off food.

"It's Monday, I should be in history right now," said Maika. "And I don't mind history. Like, imagine how four kids might have walked along this exact path five hundred years ago," she continued. "Four teenagers wearing baggy shirts and, I don't know, woollen trousers or skirts. On their way to school maybe."

"My ancestors were in India," Suravi said.

"And my granddad was Russian," I said.

"OK, I'm a bit Scottish," said Maika. "I think. But I'm not saying these kids were actually related to us."

"Would they have had any food with them?" Barney asked. "Bread and cheese, maybe? And apples."

It was a weird idea, walking in the five-hundred-year-old footsteps of kids who'd gone before us, but I liked it. It made me feel like I was outside my body, looking down at us from up high, like a seagull watching four friends trudging across a field. Four friends walking through history.

We walked and walked. We passed the occasional bench. We'd spot a headland up ahead and think we'd be able to see Robin Hood's Bay when we'd passed it. But no, just more path, the Cleveland Way stretching on and on for ever. We went down some steps and over a stream, then up some steps and carried on. Being so hungry was almost a good thing because it kept us going. The only way to get food was finding Uncle Universe and asking him for some.

So we kept walking. On and on.

And I knew it was time to tell them that I was planning to move in with Uncle Universe. But I didn't want to. I'd already abandoned them once, in Scarborough. This would feel like abandoning them again.

"I don't understand," Barney said, "how a man like that wakes up in the morning and has his Cheerios or whatever, and then somehow gets on with his day, when his day involves stealing dogs and taking other people's money. How does he do that?"

He just blurted it out. No one had spoken for a while. It sounded like it had been going round and round in his head. I felt like telling Barney, *It's because he's basically like cancer*, but I didn't want to bring the mood down even further.

"Why is he stealing dogs anyway?" Maika wondered.

"Owners offer a reward," Barney said bleakly. "So he says he found their dog and he gets the cash. Or if it's pedigree, he can sell it on for thousands."

"Some people are just horrible," Suravi said in a surprisingly harsh voice. I glanced at her. Her nostrils were flaring, her teeth gritted, and I wondered if she was thinking about the Disney princess who'd called her "Subaru".

"Some people are horrible on purpose," Maika said, "and some people are horrible by accident."

I had a feeling she was talking about me, but I didn't say anything. We walked through endless trees, and I heard water tumbling and splashing over rocks. We passed a sign that read:

Cleveland Way
Public Footpath

It was reassuring, and it didn't tell us to beware of anything. We walked and walked and walked.

"Walking's pretty boring," Suravi said eventually.

"I'm never going to walk anywhere ever again after this," Barney said. "I'm going to keep an electric scooter by my bed, get on it when I get up, and not get off it till bedtime."

We reached a bench with a panel next to it with a lot of information that told us we were at Ravenscar. I got my map out, tried to read it while I walked, and nearly tripped and fell. "We're almost there!" I said, pointing at the map. No one bothered to look at it. Too tired, too hungry. We passed a house with a garage and big windows. They must have a great view from those windows.

We turned away from the sea, walked alongside a high hedge and then we were on a paved path that took us to an actual road.

"Wait," I said. "Is this right? The Cleveland Way shouldn't be on a road, should it?"

We were at the gates of a drive. A sign said:

Raven Hall Hotel

"Let's go in," said Suravi. She yawned, rubbing her stomach. "We can find someone to ask where the Cleveland Way's gone."

"And maybe we can beg for some food," said Barney.

We went down the drive, past hydrangea bushes with big, fat, faded blue and pink flowers. The hotel was in front of us, with a wide green lawn beside it and some lodges on the other side of the lawn. There were wooden tables on the grass, where people could have meals or drinks.

No one was there.

But there was a tray on one of the tables.

And on the tray there was a full English breakfast.

TWENTY-THREE

You could tell just by looking at it that it was the best breakfast ever.

We stared at it with big eyes and open mouths. There was a dish of muesli and a jug of milk. There was a plate of crispy, pink bacon, two fried eggs, two sausages, a little lake of beans, a shiny disc of black pudding, and two triangular hash browns. There was a rack of white and brown toast, and a dish of butter next to a little pot of marmalade, a plate with a big flaky croissant and a sticky pastry with an orange apricot in the middle of it. There was a clementine, there was orange juice and there was a cafetière with a coffee cup beside it.

I was literally licking my lips and so were Suravi, Barney, Maika and Milo.

The sun was higher in the sky now, and the tray was sitting in a pool of shining golden light. If there wasn't dramatic church music playing, it certainly felt like there should be because this was a miracle.

We just stood there, staring. I was dribbling a bit.

No one was around. Someone must have been taking it to one of the lodges. Maybe they'd forgotten something and gone back into the hotel.

"Guys," Barney whispered. There was a little tremble in his voice.

He took a step forward.

"We can't steal it," I said, but my tone was doubtful. I didn't even convince myself.

"We can, though," Suravi muttered.

Maika was looking from the hotel to the lodge to the breakfast. "We have to make a decision," she said. "We have to…"

And then she stopped talking, because Barney was running.

He ran to the table and picked up the tray, at which point a woman in black trousers and a white shirt came out of the hotel and shouted at him.

"Hey!"

He ran.

"Hey, stop!"

He didn't stop.

He didn't run back towards us, he ran down the lawn with that tray with a huge breakfast on it, complete with drinks and a jug of milk and a clementine, with Milo barking at his heels. We looked at each other … and then we ran after him and the woman ran after us.

This was ludicrous. We were running *into* the hotel's garden… Where were we going to go? And Barney wasn't running fast because of the tray.

He dropped the clementine and I picked it up without slowing down.

He dropped the milk jug. I didn't pick that up.

He dropped a sausage and Milo got that.

"Come back!" the woman shouted.

But Barney didn't come back. In fact, he ran faster because he'd seen a door in the wall. He angled towards it. Which was all very well, but if the door was locked, we'd be trapped. We'd get caught, and I'd probably never find Uncle Universe, all because of bacon and eggs.

It wasn't locked.

Maika darted ahead of Barney and she yanked the door open, so he ran straight through it, followed by Milo (with a sausage in his mouth), Maika, Suravi and finally me.

"Sorry!" I shouted, panting, and slammed the door on the woman who was following us.

We went down some steps and kept running over what seemed to be a golf course, and when I looked back the woman wasn't following, she was just standing in the doorway, hands on hips, watching us.

We headed for the treeline at the edge of the golf course, and as we did so I looked out over the land curving away in front of us. I was pretty sure that this was Robin Hood's Bay and that I could see the little village itself, a triangle of white-walled houses sliding down towards the sea in a curve in the hillside.

It was just a couple of miles ahead.

We ran into the trees, Barney still holding the tray like a frantic waiter, all of us looking over our shoulders expecting to see a chef chasing after us waving a big cooking knife. Nobody came. We kept going at full speed for a bit, just to be safe, and then we sat down in the shade. Barney carefully lowered the tray, holding Milo back, and we sat around it, all of us panting. I leant against a tree trunk. Sea, bacon and grass – I had all three of my favourite smells all at once.

"OK," Suravi gasped, still getting her breath back, "we should share it out."

We all nodded and agreed, looking at the tray. The croissant was sitting in the beans, the muesli was sprinkled everywhere, the cafetière was on its side leaking coffee. And then we just started picking up food and stuffing it in our mouths; we just grabbed what we could and kept going, barely chewing, like we were in a race. I wrapped half the croissant round most of a sausage and dipped it in baked beans. It was salty and beany and soft and doughy and it was probably the nicest thing I'd ever eaten. I followed it with toast and marmalade, some dry muesli sprinkled on top and a bit of hash brown.

I washed it down with black coffee. I don't even like coffee.

In about thirty seconds all the food was gone.

I burped.

Someone farted.

"Hey!" said Maika.

"Wasn't me," said Barney.

"Well, it wasn't me," said Suravi.

One of them was lying.

I got the clementine out of my pocket and split it into four. We all chewed our segments slowly.

"That wasn't quite a Perfect Moment," said Suravi, holding her stomach, "because we had to steal the food. But I'm definitely giving them five stars on Trip Advisor."

"Maybe it wasn't a Perfect Moment," I said, "but it still goes to the top of my list of best breakfasts ever."

"Mine too," Barney said.

"We will pay, though," Maika insisted.

We all nodded.

"We'll apologize and send them money," Suravi said. "And we'll tell them they literally saved our lives."

More nodding.

"So this bay we're in," I said, pointing through the trees, "is Robin Hood's Bay. We're nearly there."

We all got up. I wanted to lie down and have a nap, I wanted to let the food I'd guzzled digest a bit, but we were so close now. So close. We walked to the edge of the trees. I didn't even need to get the map out; we could see where we were going.

I pointed at the houses sliding down towards the sea.

"It's about two miles, I reckon. Shall we?"

We left the tray with the dirty plates and stuff on the golf course where we hoped it would be seen, then we walked along the treeline until we found a track leading down a slope. We climbed over a fence at the bottom of the track, crossed a field in which some cows looked at us curiously, over another fence, and then we were back on the clifftop.

And there was the Cleveland Way. It felt like an old friend now.

Walking again. Walking, walking, walking. But this time it was different, we were enjoying it. We were taking it slowly, because we didn't want to get stitches and breakfast was heavy in our stomachs, but there was a warm breeze off the sea that smelled salty and fresh and we were all in good moods. Suravi put some music on her phone and we sang along for a bit, which was really nice till her phone died.

We were walking in pairs: me next to Suravi, Barney next to Maika, but then Barney caught up with us. He gave me a tight smile and jerked his head back. I thought about pretending I didn't get it, but there wasn't much point in that, so I slowed down and walked beside Maika, leaving Barney with Suravi.

"What's going on?" Maika whispered. "He going to ask her out?"

I stared at her. "You know about that?"

She half smiled. "I'm not blind."

And then we both stopped talking, slowed down to give them privacy, but kept watching, trying to pick up what was going on from the way they were walking, their half-turned faces, how close they were to each other.

After about three minutes, Barney hung back. Without a word, Maika moved up next to Suravi, and I found myself walking next to Barney.

"All right?" I said.

He shrugged and looked away.

So much for my good mood. Barney had been rejected and I didn't know what to say to him.

"Mate…" I began.

"It's fine," he said, then looked away again.

We trudged on, our moods suddenly lower. I had no idea what was going to happen next. I wanted to be optimistic. Phase Two of running away was nearly finished and soon I'd be knocking on Uncle Universe's door with his letter in my hand, and maybe for a moment he'd look puzzled, but then a huge smile would appear on his face as he realized it was me. That was definitely a thing that could happen.

Possibly.

But in the meantime, I was walking beside my mate

whose heart was a bit broken. I could have warned Barney that I didn't think he had much chance with Suravi, but that would have been insulting. There was an air of awkwardness and embarrassment hanging over all four of us now, and we'd run out of things to say. We were just walking, each lost in their own thoughts, none of us in a good mood.

So of course, I made it worse. I should have told them earlier but I hadn't and I'd run out of time. I had to do it now.

"Right," I announced abruptly, looking straight forward at the path ahead. "My plan is, if I find Uncle Universe and if it all goes well, I might actually, in fact, stay here. In Robin Hood's Bay. With him."

I just said it. I didn't think about it first because I knew if I thought about it, I probably wouldn't say it.

They stopped walking, so I stopped walking too.

"Yeah, we guessed," said Suravi.

I stared at her, at all of them. "You did?"

Barney sighed. "We talked about it when we thought we were going home," he said. "It was pretty obvious that's what you were thinking."

"I'm sorry," I told him, "but I just feel like it's what I need. Because I'm worried my parents are going to, you know, stifle me, and I want to get away from that, and school and my whole ordinary life."

"We're your ordinary life," Barney said quietly. "You want to get away from us?"

"No," I said. "No, but…"

I hesitated, not sure how to end that sentence. Maika filled in the silence that followed.

"If it's what you need," she said sadly, "it's what you need." She shrugged. "I think we have to support you." She looked at Barney and Suravi. "That's what friends do."

Barney looked miserable; Suravi looked cross. "Fine," she said at last. "Hope you'll have a nice life up here, without your mates."

She and Barney walked on. Maika and I followed them. I wanted to say something to Maika, I wanted to thank her, but she was looking away from me, out to sea, her eyes all squinty, and I felt like she didn't want to talk. The path was paved now, an unfriendly fence strung with barbed wire at its side, but there were red roofs ahead of us and below us.

Robin Hood's Bay.

We descended wooden steps down through the trees and talked as we went, our voices flat, as if all the hope and energy had been drained out of us.

Suravi: "So how big is this place?"

Maika: "It looks quite small."

Barney: "Will he recognize you?"

"I don't know," I said. "Yes." And, "I hope so."

This wasn't how I'd hoped to arrive, with our mood so low and our friendships frayed, as if we were giving up and going home instead of finally reaching our destination.

Red roofs and white walls. It looked a bit toytown-ish. We were at the height of the roofs now; the sea was making a noise like traffic behind the trees and there were skylights peering at us. Maybe Uncle Universe was sat in one of them having his breakfast, seeing four gloomy kids approaching his little village by the sea.

Barney paused to pick a blackberry and then, at last, stone steps past a rockery brought us down into the village itself. We came out next to a sign that said **FLAGSTAFF STEPS**.

We'd done it. We'd made it. And nobody felt even slightly happy about it.

An old lady was standing in the road. She wore a purple dress made of shiny, scratchy material, and she had lots of white hair falling down over her shoulders.

"Oh, here you are at last," she said, smiling like she was delighted to see us. "I've been expecting you."

TWENTY-FOUR

I stared at her. I took a step backwards.

She laughed. She had a dry laugh, like leaves rustling. If I'd still had my bottle of water, I might have offered her a drink.

"Your faces!" she croaked. "You look like you've seen a sea monster."

Well, she didn't look like a sea monster, but to be fair to us, she did look unusual. There was the purple dress, the waves of loose white hair, and her pale powdery face which looked a bit like my map: scribbled all over with wrinkly little lines. Her lips were pink and pursed, her nose was small and pointy and her eyes were all crinkled up. She could have been a fairy godmother.

And then there was what she'd said.

"You've been … *expecting* us?" I said. The words came out oddly hesitant and bumpy, but I couldn't help it. This was weird.

"*Nooo.*" She almost sang the word, stretching it out as if that was the most ridiculous thing she'd ever heard. She seemed to think we were hilarious. "No, no, of course I haven't been expecting you, how is that possible? I was joking, my dear. I've never set eyes on you before, foolish boy."

"Right…" I began, still hesitant.

"But," she said, raising a straight finger, "I do need your succour. Which means assistance. I'm very fortunate to have stumbled on four fine young people like yourselves and I don't for a moment believe the nonsense one hears about youths these days – about them all being rude thugs and vandals. So, allow me to ask you a small favour."

She paused and took a breath, which was fair enough because she'd been talking fast in her husky voice and barely pausing.

We all waited.

"The favour is, will you be gentlemen and ladies, and please help an ageing damsel in distress? By which I mean me." She pressed her hand against her chest, as if we might not understand who she meant unless she showed us.

"No," said Suravi. "Definitely a whole big pile of no."

The old lady stared at her.

I stared at her too. That was quick. I thought we'd discuss it at least.

"You're obviously friends with the man who stole

Milo!" Suravi said, loud, outraged, hands in the air. "Obviously!"

The woman's wrinkly face got even wrinklier as she poked her head forward like a tortoise. I'm not good at estimating ages, but I guessed she might be around one hundred and twelve. She peered at Suravi, screwing up her eyes.

"I'm friends with the *who* who stole *what*?" she rasped.

Suravi looked at us. "Why are we even wasting our time talking to her?" she said.

Maika nodded. Maika usually agrees with Suravi. Barney stared at her and then looked at me, obviously not sure what to think.

"But I'm locked out!" The woman's voice went all piping and sad. She had her hands in the air too, same as Suravi, only hers were old and wrinkly, as if she was wearing gloves that didn't fit very well.

"I'm locked out of my house and I can't get in!" All the humour had gone out of her voice, she just sounded like a confused old lady. "Won't you help me?" Her finger pointed at Suravi, shaking a little. "You and..." Her unsteady finger pointed at me. "... Milo?"

"I'm not Milo," I said. I pointed at the dog. "That's Milo."

Milo wagged his tail.

The lady nodded, as if I'd just introduced myself. "And my name is Dorothy Avery," she said. "So very pleased to meet you all. Please just help me get into my little house and then you can be on your merry way. I can offer you a piece of homemade fruit cake, or money, in return for your kind assistance."

I raised a finger. "Could you just, for a minute, wait?"

I turned to my friends, and we stepped away.

"I think she's confused," I whispered. "I don't think she's bad."

"She's lying!" Suravi hissed. But I could see a little doubt on her face.

"Even if she's lying, what can she do?" said Barney. "She's an old lady."

"You just want cake," Maika muttered.

"No I don't," he said angrily. "Don't be mean." He sighed. "But would that be so bad? Or we could use a bit of money."

"Let's help her," I said. "It won't take long."

"Bossy!" Suravi snapped.

I ignored this and turned back to Dorothy. "Where's your house?" I asked.

She smiled, lifting her chin, opening her eyes wider, suddenly looking much happier. "Call me Dottie," she said.

She took us down a narrow road between buildings. A fish-and-chip shop on the right, the back of a pub on the left, the blank white walls of houses. Uncle Universe could be in any of them. I'd only visited once, years ago. I had a feeling he lived on a long road but I wasn't sure. I knew I was close, though, so close, and yet somehow I'd stumbled into a detour. How had that happened?

We took a couple of turns and then we were going up a steep hill. It was only short, but it was the steepest hill I'd ever climbed. It was almost vertical and it was literally the last thing we needed after our epic walk. It nearly killed us. We stumbled out on to the flat eventually and paused on a small green.

"Where do you live?" I gasped.

Dottie set off again. She was a slow walker, creeping along ahead of us, confident that we'd follow. She took us round a corner. We were going uphill again now, alongside a terrace of red-brick houses set back from the road, with a line of trees behind it.

"Here," she said finally. "I live here."

We all went up some steps and through a gate into her little front garden and looked at her red-brick house as if it was something special. Which it wasn't. I still didn't think she was lying, but I was wondering why we'd just spent fifteen minutes basically walking out of Robin Hood's Bay. I'd spent all this time getting here and now I was leaving?

I didn't want to be at Dottie's house, that was the point. Not unless it turned out Uncle Universe lived next door to her. I'd lied to my parents, I'd run away from the police, I'd nearly fallen off a roof, I'd lost my friends and found them again, I'd walked for miles and miles and miles, and rescued Milo, and escaped from a dog thief, and stolen a breakfast, and disappointed my friends, but now I was in the middle of this peculiar, pointless delay.

"Look." Barney was pointing. There were big windows on the ground floor of Dottie's house and smaller windows above them. Barney was pointing at one of the smaller windows, which was open.

I stared at it. "Don't think I can fit through there," I said.

Suravi looked at Maika.

"I'm shorter than you," she said.

And then, without discussing it any more, Suravi took off her puffy green coat and dropped it on the grass. We all approached the house.

"I need a boost," she told us.

She put her foot in my laced fingers, then leant on Barney's shoulder while Maika held her hips. She had her feet on the narrow window ledge and her hands inside the little window.

"It's on some sort of latch." She twisted her head round to look at Dottie. "I might have to break it."

"Do what you must, my dear," said Dottie.

Suravi reached into her pocket and took out her throwing star. "Knew it would come in handy," she said.

She wiggled it, grunting, and there was a loud click. And then she was pulling herself up into the window, shimmying through the narrow gap with her hands in front of her like she was diving.

She fell forwards into the room, on to a sofa.

I was standing next to Dottie, who had a big, pink smile on her face.

"Oh, good girl," she said. "Like a little gymnast."

I looked at her. What was happening here? This didn't make sense. It felt as if we'd somehow taken a wrong turning when we came off the Cleveland Way and we weren't actually in Robin Hood's Bay at all. Because instead of knocking on Uncle Universe's door, I was watching Suravi break into this strange old lady's house.

And I was going right off Dottie. She was slippery – fragile and vulnerable one minute, pleased with herself and smug the next. Maybe that's how people who are roughly one hundred and twelve behave, but what had she been doing, standing there by Flagstaff Steps as if she was waiting for us? Suravi was right: she was probably lying. Wasn't she? *But why would she be lying?*

I had this whole dialogue going on in my head, trying to work out why I was doing what I was doing. Meanwhile Suravi gave us the thumbs up through the window and went off to the front door.

"Oh, isn't she a resourceful young lady?" said Dottie. "Aren't you all admirable young people?"

I was suddenly certain that we shouldn't go into Dottie's house. It felt like absolutely the wrong thing to do. In fact, it felt dangerous.

Suravi opened the front door.

"Come along, then!" Dottie said. "Homemade cake! And I absolutely insist that you accept some money for your trouble."

Suravi was standing there, waiting. Maika had picked up her coat and she and Barney were walking towards her. I was still certain that we shouldn't go into Dottie's house, certain that it was the wrong thing to do.

But Suravi was already in there, and Barney and Maika were halfway to the front door.

So I followed them.

TWENTY-FIVE

Soft green carpet in the hall, pale yellow walls. It smelled musty and sweet, like old flowers. It hadn't exactly been noisy outside, but inside there was a heavy, overwhelming hush.

"That's right," said Dottie, shutting the door behind us. "That's right, through to the lounge. Well, thank you ever so much." She clapped. She actually clapped her hands three times. "I'm *so* grateful. Now, the bathroom is at the end of the hall. Cake and juice for everyone? Make yourselves comfortable."

She went to the kitchen and Suravi looked at me and shrugged. "We might as well get some cake," she said. "And maybe some cash."

The soft green carpet continued into the lounge. I glanced around at a sofa and armchairs with puffy cushions, all in a velvety tasselled material, the colour of chocolate cake. There were lots of pottery figures on glass shelves with little lights above them. I went to the loo. It was a small pink room at the back of the house with a frosted glass window.

I was wishing I'd listened to Suravi before. *"A whole big pile of no."*

This was a distraction, obviously. It was almost like we were deliberately putting off finding Uncle Universe. Could that be it? Our group felt as fractured as it had ever been. The whole ordeal was nearly over, and I was pretty sure that none of us wanted it to end with tension and stress simmering away between us.

I had a wee, then stood at the sink washing my hands, looking at my reflection. Long hair, thin face, pouty lips twisted in a worried frown.

I marched back to the lounge. No Dottie. How long did it take to bring out some cake?

"We shouldn't bother with cake and juice!" I told them. No one was saying anything, but my voice was loud, like everyone was talking at once and I was trying to be heard. "I think we're killing time here because we're suddenly all feeling weird about each other, which is mostly my fault, and I'm sorry, but let's just go and find Uncle Universe. Now!"

Dottie came in carrying a tray with cake and plates, juice and glasses. She acted like she hadn't heard me, but she must have.

"Here we are!" she said, croakily singing the words. "How lovely to have such pleasant company. Now, you all tuck in, and I'll just pop off and find my purse. Won't be a jiffy."

She went out again and we all stared at the cake as if it might have an opinion.

"It would be rude if we just walked out now," Maika said.

Suravi nodded reluctantly. "We'll have a quick bit of cake, we'll let her give us a fiver, and then we'll go. All right?"

She gave Barney a piece. Barney prodded it, then took a bite.

And then, weirdly, we were all sitting in the lounge, on the brown sofa and the armchair, eating fruit cake and sipping juice like we were about fifty years old. I was still restless and uneasy and I was about to say something again but Suravi spoke first. She was looking at Barney.

"You're my mate," she said. "One of my best mates. You know that, don't you? I hope that's not going to change."

Barney had a mouthful of cake. He chewed slowly, looking at his shoes. Then he looked up, at Suravi. "It's not going to change," he said.

Which was nice. Embarrassing, and not entirely convincing, but nice. But as well as embarrassing and not convincing and nice, it was irrelevant, because I was still restless and uneasy, and we were still sat in Dottie's house, not looking for Uncle Universe.

I got up and went to the kitchen. Sure enough, I saw a box with a cellophane window and the words "Rich Fruit Cake" on the side. *OK, not homemade, then*, I thought. But I also saw something else. A bottle of Jameson whiskey beside the toaster. I stared at it. My stomach seemed to clench and my chest tightened. All of a sudden, it was hard to breathe. I had a very bad feeling.

I brought the box and the bottle back into the lounge, waving them like they were vital pieces of evidence.

"Jameson whiskey!' I said. 'Flat Face mentioned Jameson in Scarborough, I heard him when we were on the roof. And the cake's not homemade, it's from the Co-op. I know it doesn't prove anything, I know that, but please, I just want to go, I want to go now!'

"You're the one who wanted to come here!" Suravi said.

"Well, I changed my mind. I don't trust her!" I told her. I stared at them: Barney all worried, Maika looking thoughtful, Suravi with a puzzled frown on her face.

I couldn't help it, I felt like I couldn't stay there another minute. Dottie kept disappearing, first to the kitchen, now upstairs. Everything was taking too long.

"She's stalling," I said. "Why is she making us wait?"

Suravi shrugged. "She told us – she's getting her purse."

I shifted my weight from foot to foot. My piece of cake was on the coffee table; I'd only taken one bite. I didn't care. I couldn't remember any other time in my life when I'd had no interest in cake.

"Let's go," I repeated. "Please. I know I've let you down and I'm sorry, but please, let's just go."

They all looked at me, and then they all put down their plates. I think they could hear the urgency in my tone. I felt trapped, I felt like I might be about to have a full-on panic attack.

"Time to go," Maika said.

Barney nodded.

"All right," Suravi said.

I went straight to the front door. I didn't care about looking bossy, or whether Dottie would be offended. I just knew suddenly that I needed to get out of that house. I turned the handle and pulled. The door didn't move. I pushed. It didn't budge.

The door was locked.

Dottie had locked us in.

"Now then," she said, coming slowly down the stairs, "I do like to lock my front door. For security." She was waving a five-pound note, looking like a fairy godmother again, descending from the sky. "Look what I've got. A gift for good children."

"We'd like to go please," I squeaked, my voice vibrating with anxiety.

"Yes, yes, yes," she said, smiling happily, as if I'd just said something nice about the fruit cake. "All in good time."

"No," said Suravi. "Sorry, but we need to go now."

233

Dottie ignored this. She went into the lounge. We followed her. We didn't have much choice.

And then she turned to me, crinkly eyes staring, and there was a mean little twist to her tightly pursed lips. She wasn't smiling any more.

"Now, tell me this my dear," she said. "Where are your parents?"

I stared back at her. We all did.

"Have you run away, is that it?" Her head tilted, her rustling voice all caring. "How charming."

She looked at each of us, as if waiting for a reply, but no one spoke.

"I must say," she said, "my son is very cross with you all. *Very* cross."

I heard a car pulling up outside. I looked out of the window. It wasn't a car. It was a dirty red van.

And our creepy, flat-faced, dog-thief neighbour was getting out.

TWENTY-SIX

This was bad.

What was he going to do?

Steal Milo, for a start.

This was very bad.

He must have watched us heading off along the Cleveland Way and phoned his mum, told her to look out for us, find some way to stall us. And we'd fallen for it. Dottie was smirking, obviously delighted with herself. Barney's lips were quivering; Maika was looking at Suravi anxiously; Suravi's cheek was twitching and her eyes were darting around as if she was looking for a way out. There was no way out. Unless we broke a window or dug a tunnel or something.

Dottie went to open the front door.

About ten seconds later he was walking in. Actually, he was striding in, all eager and intense, like a boxer entering a ring. Short grey hair, flat pink face, lips pulled back showing his teeth. He jabbed his finger at us and we all flinched.

"You four," he hissed. "You've cost me. What you going to do about it?"

"Sorry about that," said Suravi. Her voice was high-pitched and shaky, but it was spiky and sarcastic too and she looked just as angry as he did. "We'll pay you back, shall we? Oh, wait, we can't – you stole all our money!"

She was so brave that she made me want to be as brave as her.

"You test me," he growled, his voice shaking as much as hers, "you will be sorry."

Milo barked at him. Maika's teeth were clenched, my hands were forming fists. There was so much anger in Dottie's little front room that it felt like everything should have been vibrating and the pottery figures should have been falling off the glass shelves. But also, I was slowly realizing none of this made sense. He was standing here, snarling at us and threatening us, but what was he actually going to do? We all knew what he looked like, we knew where he lived, we knew he'd stolen all the dogs. We were immediately going to tell the police once we got out of Dottie's house. What could he possibly do to us, all four of us together?

Milo jumped forwards, growling. We all stared down at him. His paws were splayed in front of him, claws out, his head was tilted up towards Flat Face, his little teeth were all showing and he was making a sound like a motorbike with a sore throat.

And then, suddenly, Flat Face bent down and snatched him up.

"Give him back!" Barney shouted.

Flat Face shook his head slowly, gripping Milo tightly, a hand clamped round his jaws as he squirmed. A mean smile appeared on his face. "I'm taking him," he said. "You kids say a word to the police, and bad things will happen. You understand what I'm saying?" He looked down at Milo and squeezed him so that he let out a muffled whimper. "Bad. Things."

There was a moment of silence then. Six of us standing there, in Dottie's lounge, like gunfighters. Flat Face clutching Milo, with his mum behind him; the four of us opposite, just staring, taking in what he'd said. "*Bad things will happen.*" The silence probably only lasted about two seconds before I broke it, but it felt longer.

I've never been in a fight, but my face was like stone and my fists were clenched as we faced this guy who was horrible on purpose, who was genuinely a bit like cancer. I think I was actually quivering. "Is your name Steven?" I asked.

He stared at me. "How…?"

Suravi laughed nervously, but I wasn't even surprised. It just seemed right.

"OK, Steve," I hissed. "The thing you don't get is, I've got nothing to lose. You know what I've got hanging over me? Death. Actual death. So you – you're nothing."

I mean, it was a bit melodramatic, yes, and it clearly just confused flat-faced Steve, who looked puzzled, but it sounded pretty cool to me. I'd definitely had enough of being scared and running away from this man. I was wondering what to say next but then Barney totally stepped on my moment.

"And me!" he yelled. "I've got nothing to lose too!"

Which obviously wasn't true at all, but he didn't care, because then he roared, or, actually, he *ROARED!* It was like a battle cry, there were no words, it was just a raging explosion of sound, and at the same time Barney himself was exploding, flying forwards, both feet off the ground, grabbing for Milo like a rugby player doing a desperate last-ditch tackle.

It turned out timid, teddy-bearish Barney was the bravest person in the room.

It got a bit confusing after that. Me, Suravi and Maika all followed Barney, charging forwards, not like rugby players, more like completely out-of-control wrestlers, and Milo, barking wildly, bit Steve on his flat pink cheek. Our fractured, fraught little group were together again, entirely in harmony, united in one furious, chaotic purpose.

We all ended up on the floor, on the soft green carpet,

tangled and grappling, yelling and gasping, while Dottie kept shouting "Stop it at once!" over our heads.

My face was jammed into someone's stomach, and I didn't even know whose it was, but I looked up and saw that Dottie had grabbed one of the bigger pottery figures – it was a shepherd wearing a wide brown hat with a sheep beside him – and she looked like she was about to drop it on my head.

Was this how my whole (partly sane, partly irrational) plan to find Uncle Universe was going to end? With an old lady smashing a piece of pottery on my head?

There was a loud rapping on the front door.

TWENTY-SEVEN

Dottie looked out of the window, then she whirled round and glared at us, still lying on her carpet like broken gymnasts.

"You don't say a word!" Her voice was raspy and urgent. "Not one word!"

She left the lounge and we could hear her talking in a nervous, shaky voice. She said something about being busy, asked someone what they wanted, but before they could answer Barney got up and looked out of the window. And then he yelled, "We're in here!"

Dottie came back in, looking furious, followed by two police officers, a big burly man and a shorter, dark-haired woman. They wore open-necked white shirts with thick black vests over them. They had radios on their shoulders and handcuffs on their hips. I couldn't quite work out whether I was relieved or frustrated as the two of them walked into the room. Flat-faced Steve was surely going to get arrested, but this was the end. Running away was over.

I was never going to find Uncle Universe now.

We all got to our feet, panting and groaning. Steve's shirt was torn and his face was bleeding, and Barney's eye was red and swollen. He was holding Milo close to his chest, as if he thought someone might still try to grab him.

"So," said the woman, looking at each of us carefully, "who would like to tell me exactly what's going on?"

"Can I offer you a drink?" asked Dottie. Her voice was still nervous and shaky like her throat was too tight. She was probably trying to act as if everything was normal, but she was gripping her pottery shepherd as if she wanted to throttle it. "Tea or coffee? A glass of water?"

"He stole my dog and a whole lot of other dogs!" Barney shouted suddenly. Everybody jumped. He was pointing at Flat Face. "And he just tried to steal him again!"

"And she locked us in," Maika said, pointing at Dottie, her voice almost as loud as Barney's.

"And we've run away," I said in a much smaller voice. "It's all my fault."

The woman police officer had a short ponytail, and she was tapping her hat against her leg while she looked at all of us. Her eyebrows were pressing together and her forehead was wrinkling a bit, as if we were unusual and worth considering closely. She looked at Flat Face.

'Steven Avery?' she said.

He nodded reluctantly.

She gestured towards Barney's eye.

"Did you do that to him?"

"No," he snapped.

"Yes!" said Barney.

She looked at her mate and nodded. And then her mate arrested Flat Face. He arrested him! It was just like TV: he was arrested on suspicion of assault and theft and he was put in handcuffs and told that he didn't have to say anything.

He glared at me while the handcuffs were going on. His lips were pressed together hard, his nostrils flaring, his pink face even pinker than usual, a dribble of blood running down his cheek. I wanted to look away but I didn't, I looked right back at him and I kept my head still, my gaze steady. Barney, Suravi and Maika were all staring at him too. And suddenly all the air seemed to go out of him, his shoulders slumped and his head dropped like he was deflating.

The male police officer led him away. He took him out of Dottie's lounge, out of the house and out of our lives. I think all four of us wanted to literally cheer, but we managed not to. Instead we just looked at each other and grinned.

We watched through the window as he was marched to the police car, his hands handcuffed behind his back, his eyes on his feet. I could have watched that all day long.

"You're making a mistake!" Dottie squeaked, her dry voice high-pitched and angry.

"Right," said the female police officer in a brisk, efficient voice. She looked at Dottie. "I'd like you to sit down please. I'll have some questions for you in a moment."

Dottie looked like she wanted to object. She opened her mouth and closed it again, glared at us, then sank into a velvety brown armchair, still clutching her pottery shepherd.

The female police officer had a small, sharp face. Sharp cheekbones, nose and chin. Sharp eyes, which were now pointed at me. I met them briefly then looked at her knees, which was a lot easier. They weren't sharp. "My name's Claire," she said. "Hello. Why don't we all sit down and have a chat while we wait for another police car to arrive?"

Barney's face was bright red, and he wasn't quite shouting, but he was definitely loud. "What d'you mean, another police car? You're not going to arrest us too, are you?"

Milo barked.

Claire gave him a stern look. It was the sort of look Miss Ahmed gives you when she catches you talking in class. "What I'd like now," she said quietly, "is a nice, calm conversation. No raised voices necessary."

Barney bit his lip. He looked embarrassed. He put Milo

on the floor and sat on the brown sofa. Suravi and Maika sat beside him, and I sat on a brown armchair. It looked like we were ready for more cake, more juice, and another little chat about Suravi and Barney's friendship.

"So," Claire continued, "we traced a caravan full of dogs to a Steven Avery. In the process of looking for him, I come to visit his mother and find that World War Three has broken out."

Her eyes moved over each of us. She'd dropped the stern look. "I'd love to know what the four of you are up to, please." She'd dropped the brisk, efficient tone as well; she just sounded genuinely curious now.

But no one spoke. There was a long, embarrassing silence. Of all the silences over the last few days, this was the most awkward. Dottie had a clock on a shelf which looked like it was made of stone and I was glad she hadn't dropped it on my head. It ticked loudly. Or maybe it just seemed loud in the heavy, overwhelming hush.

Barney, Suravi and Maika all looked at me, so Claire looked at me too. I counted six ticks.

Claire perched on the arm of another armchair like she didn't want to get too comfortable.

"What's your name?" she asked me.

"Jasper," I told her.

"OK, Jasper, how about you start at the beginning?" Her mouth had a small, amused curl at the corner. "After that, you can tell me about the middle and then you can finish up at the end: how you came to be right here, on a brown armchair in Robin Hood's Bay, talking to me."

Claire seemed nice. Sharp-faced and sharp-eyed, but kind. Still, I didn't speak. Because "start at the beginning" isn't as simple as all that. What was the beginning anyway? Was it the three of us on the roof of the shed on Thursday, or Suravi throwing the chair at school on Friday, which led to me walking out? Or was it the four of us back on the roof of the shed that evening?

It was probably none of those things. It was probably me in the doctor's office with my parents. The doctor sitting next to her desk in a white coat, eyes sliding from my parents to me then back to my parents. A milky-white scan on her computer screen. Her voice had been all cool and reassuring, like Claire's, while she'd said a lot of stuff I hadn't understood. But then she'd used the word "malignant", and my mum had started crying.

I didn't want to sit here and tell Claire about that. Why would I tell her about that? The whole point of running away was to not think about that.

Also, Claire had said "the end" was right here, on the brown armchair. And actually, it turned out I wasn't quite ready for this to be the end. Not yet, not when I was so close.

So I didn't say anything.

"They've run away," Dottie snapped, sounding impatient suddenly, and angry. "And they broke into my house! It's them you should be arresting, not my son."

Suravi looked at her. I looked at Suravi. Her fists were clenching, her shoulders were tensing, and I was worried by her face. It had gone tight, lips pulled back, teeth gritted: the same face she'd had on when she threw the chair in the canteen. I was about to say something, but as I watched her I saw her take a breath, I saw her shoulders slowly lowering and her fists slowly unclenching.

Claire looked at Dottie. "Actually, I will have that tea, thanks."

Dottie hesitated. It was obvious Claire was getting rid of her, but she could hardly refuse to go. She did a smile that looked completely false, as if someone had explained to her how to smile and she hadn't really got it.

"All right," she croaked, and she got up, finally put her pottery shepherd back on the shelf, and left the room.

Claire looked at us. "Did you break into this house?" she asked.

"No!" we all said simultaneously, voices vibrating with outrage.

Claire nodded and looked at me again. "Tell you what, Jasper," she said, "I'll start. We have a report concerning four young people behaving suspiciously in York on Saturday, which I assume is you lot. We have CCTV of you arriving in Scarborough the same day, there was the dog business on the Cleveland Way last night, a theft of a breakfast at the Raven Hall Hotel this morning, and we have a collection of very concerned parents." She raised her eyebrows, that small smile still in place. "You're not exactly low profile, you four, are you?"

It turned out they knew a lot more than I'd thought they knew. Apparently, everything about Claire was sharp (apart from her knees).

"We were always going to pay for the breakfast," Suravi muttered. She was still cross, but she was controlling it.

"And we didn't break in, she asked us to help her, and she gave us cake!" said Maika.

"Her son – he didn't just steal Milo and all the other dogs, he stole our money too." Barney's voice was all husky with outrage, but he managed not to shout. "Fifty-nine pounds and eighty-two pence, and our bank cards!"

"We haven't done anything wrong!" Suravi said. "Apart from taking the breakfast," she added limply. "Sorry about that."

Claire nodded as though she understood perfectly.

I raised my hand. And then I felt silly for raising my hand. "Can I go to the loo?" I asked.

Claire smiled. "Of course you can."

I walked down the hall to the little pink loo. I locked the door and then, without pausing, without thinking about it, I opened the frosted window wide, got up on the loo seat and climbed out, crouching, scraping my back on the top of the window.

And then I jumped to the ground and sprinted to the trees as if a hell–demon was after me.

TWENTY-EIGHT

About five minutes later, Claire stepped out of the back door. She looked at the window I'd climbed through then stood with her back to the house and scanned the area.

I was hiding in the trees, squatting down behind a bush. I was pretty sure she couldn't see me, but I crouched down lower just in case. A small bug went up my nostril, and I blew it out. She stood there, looking around, shaking her head. I thought she might actually be muttering to herself. Dottie joined her, scowling, and the two of them waited there for a bit, side by side like bad-tempered reality show judges. Then they went back in.

I got up and walked along the edge of the little strip of trees, staying out of sight. It curved round at the end of the terrace so I could see the road. My chest felt tight, my eyes were darting around. My parents were definitely either on their way already or would be very soon, along with

Maika's mum and Suravi and Barney's parents. I needed to get moving, but first I had to see what was going to happen to my friends. A new police car was arriving, so I crouched down again.

My plan was to wait for the police to leave. Then I'd have one last chance to find Uncle Universe.

After another few minutes Dottie came out of the front door, Claire behind her with a different, bored-looking male police officer. Suravi, Barney, Maika and Milo were walking between them. None of them were in handcuffs. They'd probably get driven to a police station in Whitby or Scarborough and our parents would all show up there. I just had to wait for them to go.

That was the plan. But what happened next surprised me.

Barney suddenly totally lost it.

He yelled something at Dottie and jabbed his finger at her face while Milo jumped around him and barked like a wild thing. Claire and her mate tried to get between them and Suravi literally held him back. It looked like the two of them had lost their minds and were doing some very strange dance. It was weird because, if you'd asked me, I'd totally have expected no-impulse-control Suravi to lose her temper, like she almost did in the house, and timid Barney to stay out of it. But that wasn't what was happening, it was the opposite.

Barney and Suravi staggered around, while Claire and

her mate tried to calm things down, and now Dottie was yelling too – something about her son and feral kids – and the whole lot of them looked like a drunk crowd you might see outside a pub.

And then I realized Maika was backing away.

Just a few steps.

Just a few more steps.

And then suddenly she turned and ran.

She sprinted towards the trees.

Towards me.

The male police officer spotted her and started to run after her, but Milo, brilliant Milo, barked and ran right into his legs, so he stumbled and fell briefly to his knees. Maika had a good start anyway because Barney and Suravi had been doing such a great job of distracting everyone. I stood up and waved wildly as she burst into the trees and then we ran together, neck and neck, like it was Sports Day again, like we were racing each other ahead of everyone else, each desperate to beat the other. I glanced at Maika and found she was looking at me, and we grinned, like we were still best mates. We jumped over a root and a pile of leaves, skidded down a dusty track then veered off, back into the trees. But the cop was there. I looked over my shoulder. He'd made up some of the gap and he wasn't looking bored any more.

"Come back!" he yelled.

Does that ever work? We didn't come back, obviously, we

only ran faster. I looked over my shoulder again, worried that he was getting closer, because me and Maika were the quickest in Sports Day at Hazelwood Primary, but he was an adult, and he was fit and fast. He was going to catch up with us… I was panting already, so was Maika, and he was definitely going to catch up.

But then, all of a sudden, he was flying through the air, horizontal, arms stretched out like Superman.

For a wild moment I was scared. Is that a thing, flying cops? That's not something they can do, is it? And then he landed with a loud thump and an angry shout and he just lay there for a moment, sprawled on the ground, before he gingerly started to get up, shaking his head and wincing.

Maika and I slid down a slope, out of the trees and back on to the street, then off it again immediately in case Claire came along in her police car. Down a side road, round a corner, round another, till we finally stopped, hands on our knees, gasping, laughing a bit, hardly able to speak.

"I won," Maika panted.

"No way!" I gasped.

We were in an alley, leaning on a wall with gates to back yards spaced along it.

"They were brilliant," I said. "Barney and Suravi."

Maika nodded. "It was Barney's idea. He said he'd start screaming and Suravi should try and calm him down, while I ran for it. I think he was worried Suravi might genuinely lose her temper, might use that throwing star or something."

"I can't believe they did that for me. Best friends ever."

I said that and then paused, realizing it was slightly awkward. Saying that in front of Maika. "I mean all of you," I said. "Obviously. You as well."

She ignored this and took her bag off her shoulder. She dug into it and pulled out her pink denim jacket with the white panels. "Put this on," she said.

I stared at it. "Why?"

"Because from behind we'll look like two girls, so maybe they won't stop us."

That didn't sound very likely, but it was worth a try. I pulled it on over my sweaty blue T-shirt, letting my hair hang over the collar at the back. "How do girls walk?" I asked.

"All quick and light, like the ground's hot," she told me, "and you don't want to touch it."

I stared at her. "You're joking, right?"

She looked at me like I was literally the slowest person she'd ever met. "Of course I'm joking, fool! Girls walk like boys walk: one foot in front of the other."

"OK," I said. "OK, we need to go straight to Uncle Universe before it's too late." I went to get my phone, and then froze with my hands in my pockets. Because I still had the caravan phone, but that was useless. My own phone was on the table in the flat in Scarborough. And it had Uncle Universe's address on it.

I told Maika.

"All right," she said in a quivery voice that was trying to sound calm but wasn't doing a very good job. "All right, don't panic. Think!"

"Oh, think," I said. "Good idea, thanks, that would never have occurred to me!"

"Fine," she said. "If you're going to be sarcastic, we might as well give up. Is that what you want to do?"

She was right.

I had to remember.

We stood there, in the narrow alley. A concrete path with scrubby grass on either side. A seagull squealed up above us. There was a sickly smell of garbage from the gate we were next to. My shoulder was throbbing again. Maika was staring at me. I put my hand over my eyes; my face was screwed up.

Was this where my quest was going to end?

"Cliff?" I muttered. "Yes, Cliff Road!" I shouted it triumphantly, then hesitated. "No, that doesn't sound right. Cliff Street? Cliff Lane?"

Maika had her phone out. "OK," she said. "There's a Cliff Terrace."

"Yes!" I said. And then, "I think so."

She put it into her maps app. "Says it's eight minutes' walk," she told me. "This way."

TWENTY-NINE

So we walked, trying to stay off the main road, while I kept thinking about the address. *Cliff Terrace, Cliff Terrace...* I was pretty sure that was it. But what number was it? Was it a number at all? Perhaps it was a house name? And how many houses would there be on Cliff Terrace?

I had my hands in the pockets of Maika's pink denim jacket. I stopped thinking about the address and started wondering if I looked like a girl. I doubted it. Was it possible Maika was just getting me to wear it as a joke? Maybe she'd take a picture when I wasn't looking and send it to our whole year. No, that wasn't fair, she wouldn't do that, because here she was, with me, when she didn't have to be.

But we weren't talking to each other. She was just walking along next to me in silence and I started thinking about what I'd blurted out a minute ago, about Suravi and

Barney. "*Best friends ever*." I remembered our conversation on the beach in Scarborough. Me saying, "Sorry"; her saying, "You don't sound sorry." And she'd been right, because I hadn't understood, and I still didn't.

I wanted "*Best friends ever*" to be true, I really did, but there was still this knotty, scratchy awkwardness between us. Because even now, after being with her all weekend, I still didn't understand why she'd given me such a hard time last year.

We'd been walking nearly five minutes now and neither of us had said a word, apart from Maika muttering, "This way," every now and then. We were nearly there. We were finally nearly there, right on the verge of at least getting to Uncle Universe's road and hopefully finding his actual house and then finding him.

But I put a hand on Maika's arm and stopped her.

She looked at me. "What?" she said.

I looked right back at her. "I think we have to talk," I told her.

"Now?" she said.

I nodded.

"But..." she began.

"No," I said. "Now."

She sighed. "If it's about 'Best friends ever'," she said, "don't worry about it. Look, this is the road, right here."

Cliff Terrace was a worryingly long road lined by small houses on each side with neat lawns and gravel driveways.

I had no idea how we were going to find Uncle Universe's house, but for now, I didn't care.

"I want you to know that you're all my best friends," I told her. "Barney and Suravi, and you. Definitely you too, Maika. You've literally saved my life and here you are now, still with me. You were going to tell me on the beach, but we got interrupted..." I hesitated, looked down at the pavement, looked up again. "So please, tell me what happened last year."

She hesitated too. I wasn't sure she was going to answer at all but then, finally, she said something I didn't expect.

"I never even liked dolls."

I opened my mouth, closed it again.

Her lips twisted upwards into a smile. "You looked exactly like a goldfish when you did that."

I decided not to answer.

She nodded, like I'd said something interesting. "I never liked dolls, but I bought a Barbie on eBay, around the beginning of Year 10. She had pigtails down to her waist. I think I had this idea that I could tell her my worries and she'd sort of comfort me. Because remember: my dad had left, Andi had gone to university, and my mum was busy. But I put her on a shelf over my bed and she just sat there and stared at me, and I felt like she didn't even like me. So I bought another, and then another. There was one in riding gear, there was a doctor, a mermaid, a princess. I ended up with nine of them, all lined up on the shelf, and I got that same feeling with all of them. They didn't like me."

I didn't open and close my mouth this time, but I was still having trouble understanding.

Maika bent down and picked up an empty crisp packet. "Every evening," she said, "I'd sit down with my diary and write a list of everything I'd done wrong that day, while those nine Barbies sat there on the shelf, staring. Silently judging me. There was always plenty to write. Things I'd said, things I hadn't said, things I'd done, things I hadn't done. Picking up litter, for instance." She waved the crisp packet at me, like it was evidence: Walkers, cheese and onion. "We had an assembly one day about plastics and pollution and litter, and how it's all basically out of control, and after that I just … I got a bit obsessed. I'd come home from school with armfuls of rubbish. So I'd write 'STOP PICKING UP LITTER THIS IS NOT NORMAL!!' in my diary, but it didn't make any difference, I couldn't stop."

I shook my head. "Sorry," I murmured.

"You saw me collecting rubbish in the playground one day and you said, 'What you doing, you nutter?' and everyone laughed. And that sort of flicked a switch. In my diary that night I wrote 'I HATE JASPER!' I think I was mostly angry with myself, but I turned it all on you."

I thought about nearly climbing into my mum's wardrobe and sleeping on the floor under the bed in Scarborough. Suravi throwing the chair. Barney sometimes seeming to prefer books and animals to people. I had a feeling it might be quite easy to be a bit different, a bit not normal.

"I'm really sorry," I said again.

While she was talking, she'd been partly looking at her feet, partly over my shoulder, but now at last she stared right at me. And she smiled.

"You sound sorry," she said.

"I think," I said slowly, "sometimes we're all a bit unhappy and a bit strange. Probably."

She gave me a thoughtful look, like she guessed I was thinking about myself, but she just nodded.

"But also," I said, "I think you should get rid of all those dolls."

"I already have," she told me. "First I told Suravi what I was doing, then I told Andi, then I got some help." She shrugged. "Turns out talking about your feelings instead of squashing them down and hiding them is actually quite a good thing."

She gave me another thoughtful look. I just nodded.

"I gave most of them to a charity shop," she continued. "But I kept one as a sort of reminder."

I was going to ask her why she'd bothered to keep one, but before I could, three things happened all at the same time:

1. Maika took the Barbie in the flowery dress out of her bag to show me.
2. A front door opened near us and a mum came out with a little girl in a pushchair.
3. Down at the other end of Cliff Terrace, a police car appeared, turning slowly on to the road and then stopping while, presumably, whoever was in there looked straight at us.

THIRTY

The Barbie in her flowery dress was sandy and her hair was dirty and straggly, but she still stared right at us, with her confident smile and her dead eyes.

"This is Darcy," Maika said, as if she hadn't seen the police car creeping its way towards us. "I always thought she looked like the meanest of the Barbies."

I nodded. "She does look mean. Maybe you should call her Steve instead." I glanced down the road at the police car. It was still moving, nosing slowly towards us, like a shark. "But right now, we've gotta run."

Maika ignored this. "It hurt when you called me a nutter," she told me. "I thought you were my friend." I looked at her, feeling awful, and she looked right into my eyes, calm and steady. and it was suddenly a Moment. Not a Perfect one but a Significant one, as if the world had stopped all around us. I forgot about the police and even

Uncle Universe. I just wanted to keep looking into her eyes. "I really liked you," she said.

"I really liked you too," I told her. I swallowed. "And then I didn't. But now I do again."

She leant forward. "You've been having a hard time," she whispered. "And I reckon your thinking's been a bit disorganized. But that's all right. You're OK, Jasper."

And then she kissed me, lightly, on the lips.

My thinking was definitely disorganized at that point. So was my heart. And I was having trouble breathing.

She stepped away, smiling. "So I'm going to run now," she said. She put Darcy into my hands. "You stay here, give this to that little girl."

She nodded towards the mum who was coming out of her gate with her daughter in the pushchair.

"I've got you, Jasper," she said finally, and then, before I could speak, before I could react, before I could do or say anything, she turned and sprinted away, down the middle of Cliff Terrace.

Maika. She'd provided the flat which made the whole trip possible, she'd built an indestructible sandcastle with me, she'd listened and understood when I explained about Uncle Universe, she'd even seemed to get it when I said I wanted to stay in Robin Hood's Bay. And now she'd run off to draw the police away. So I finally understood what that ache in my chest meant – the one I felt when I was watching her singing in York. And I knew why it hurt so much when she suddenly seemed to hate me.

I touched my lips, watching her disappear.

The police car sped up. I literally shook myself. It was hard to think – because my thinking was disorganized – but I had to think. I said "Hello" to the mum who was walking towards me, then crouched, my back to the road, and asked the little girl if she liked my Barbie.

I looked up at the mum. "Can she have it? I'm too old for it."

The mum looked confused. Why was this boy in pink denim giving her little girl a doll? But the girl looked delighted.

"Can I have her?" she squeaked.

I didn't know what was happening behind me. Was the police car stopping? Or was it going after the runner, ignoring the long-haired girl in pink denim chatting to the family on the pavement?

The mum shrugged. "Sure. What do you say?"

"Thank you!" said the girl. And then, "Her hair's dirty."

I smiled. "Maybe you can wash it."

I stood up as the mum went on her way, and the girl started singing to her new doll. I turned round slowly, cautiously. The road was empty. Maika's plan had worked. She'd distracted the police, and in doing so, had given me one last chance to find Uncle Universe.

There was a whole new Maika in my head now. She used to be my mate, then I basically hated her, but now ... now I really badly wanted to see her again.

But my time was running out.

I started jogging down Cliff Terrace, checking house names and numbers, hoping I'd be struck by inspiration.

This was really it. My mum and dad were almost certainly on their way, the police had Barney and Suravi, they'd probably soon have Maika, and they were still searching for me. But I was so nearly there. Uncle Universe might just be a few steps from here.

I jogged along, trying to check out both sides of the road at once, still racking my brains for the address. I was pretty sure it was a house name, not a number. Something to do with the sea? No ... but was it something to do with holidays? Sand? Sun? Halfway down Cliff Terrace on the left-hand side I saw a wooden gate with a little plaque on it.

"Sunnyside Cottage" was written on the plaque in bright yellow.

It was just another small house with a neat lawn and a gravel driveway, like all the others. I stood outside it, looking, half remembering. This was it.

SUNNYSIDE COTTAGE
CLIFF TERRACE

263

I was sure that that's what I'd seen in the old address book, I was sure it was the picture I'd taken on my phone.

My chest was suddenly so tight that I could hardly breathe.

I walked up the drive, gravel crunching under my feet. The door was bright red and it had a shiny brass lion's face on it with a knocker in its mouth. I lifted it and knocked twice. No sound of anyone moving inside. I pressed my ear up close to the door. Nothing. I shifted my weight, nervous, bouncing a little on my toes, waiting.

He wasn't answering his door.

I noticed a bell so I pushed it, but it was one of those bells where you can't hear it ring inside so you're not sure if it's working or not. I waited a few seconds, listening again, looking over my shoulder, looking up and down the street, then I lifted the knocker and this time I gave three hard raps on the door.

The sharp, angry noise seemed to echo down the street. But there was still no sound from inside. There were a couple of big windows next to the door, so I stepped off the path and looked in. There was a stove in an alcove in one wall, a big TV on another, books. But no one there.

Was this how my quest was going to end?

It was Monday morning, so even if Uncle Universe lived here, he was probably at work. Maybe if the original plan had succeeded, if my money hadn't been stolen and I'd got a cab on Sunday, maybe he would have been here.

I walked away.

What choice did I have? If I sat outside the door and waited for him, sooner or later Mum would work out why I was in Robin Hood's Bay, and the police would come and check for me here. Then they'd find me, sitting on the doorstep like a lost dog, waiting for someone who was probably never coming.

There was nothing else I could do.

I'd failed. I'd walked all the way from Scarborough. I'd been scared and hungry and in pain. I was achy and blistery and actually limping now. My friends had all been arrested. And after all that, I'd totally failed.

I just walked, I had no idea where I was going. My hands were stuffed into my pockets and I was mostly looking at the pavement. Dawdling. For the first time since Saturday, I didn't have a destination in mind, I had nowhere to be. Phase Two was finished and there was no Phase Three.

Maybe I was following my nose, the whiff of sea air, but I went back down that almost vertical hill and I realized I was approaching the beach. So I walked between tall buildings and old stone walls, down the cobbled slipway and on to damp sand the colour of cardboard. The tide was out. A long way out. I could hardly see the sea. Channels of water threaded between seaweedy rocks. There were green hills in one direction and cliffs in the other. I headed for the cliffs and when I reached the foot of them, I took off Maika's jacket, dropped it on the sand,

and sat on it. Then I lay down with my bag as a pillow and stared up at the sky.

There is no Phase Three.

Was that true, though? If Phase One of running away was taking the train to Scarborough, and Phase Two was getting to Robin Hood's Bay, maybe it was time to invent a Phase Three. Which would be proper running away, not just running away for beginners. I'd get a train in York and go wherever it took me, to London maybe, hundreds of miles away from my parents and school and that doctor in that office looking at the milky-white scan on her screen.

I closed my eyes. I was on my own on a chilly beach under a grey sky. I'd lost all my friends, and I was in big trouble with my parents, the police and school.

And I had cancer.

Steve.

No, not Steve.

Cancer.

THIRTY-ONE

My eyes were shut and my fingers were digging into the grainy wet sand. I could hear the distant shouts of children and a car alarm which briefly wailed back in the village. The sky had been grey when I shut my eyes but now I could feel weak sun on my face. I was trying to think seriously about Phase Three, which would involve being alone in London. It would be Suravi's version of running away – a scuzzy flat, a job. And maybe instead of Uncle Universe I could find a really good London doctor who could tell me something different about what was wrong with me. "Turns out it's not cancer after all. You've just sprained your shoulder!" I didn't have money for a train to London, but I could probably hide in the loo all the way.

My face got cool, suddenly. I opened my eyes. There was a man standing over me. His shadow was on my face and the sun was behind him, so he looked all hazy and dark. My stomach tightened. Was it, somehow, God knows how, was it our creepy, flat-faced neighbour?

I sat up, crinkling my eyes, trying to make out the man's features.

"Don't stare at the sun," he said. "Bad idea."

He moved to the side, out of the dazzle, and crouched down beside me.

"Jasper?" he said.

I stared at him. I'm really not good at ages, but he looked like he might be about the same age as my mum, which meant he was somewhere in his forties. He was wearing light blue shorts and a red V-neck T-shirt with a Tardis on it. He had long, dark brown hair like mine and a long face too, a big nose, and curious, hazel eyes which looked a bit like Mum's eyes.

"Uncle Universe?" I said.

He raised his eyebrows.

"I mean, Harvey. Uncle Harvey?"

He nodded. "That's me." He sat down on the sand beside me. "Been looking for you, Jasper."

I nodded back at him, and suddenly to my embarrassment my eyes were wet. "I've been looking for you too." My voice broke on the last word.

He smiled. "Hey," he said. "Hey, now."

He put his arms round me and hugged me. We stayed like that for a bit, my face pressed into his T-shirt, my shoulders shaking, his stubbly chin on the top of my head. I smelled salty sea air, and something herby, which must have been his aftershave. And then he finally let go of me and I sniffed and wiped my eyes while he tactfully looked out at the sea. When I was ready, I said, "How did you find me?"

"Got a pretty frantic call from your mum, went out searching high and also low," he said. He checked his watch. "I reckon we've got about an hour till your folks get here. Fancy an ice cream?"

"Actually," I told him, "I'm quite hungry."

The piece of fish was wrapped in thick golden batter, and it was bigger than my plate. There was a pile of chips next to it which smelled so strongly of vinegar that my nose wrinkled up, a pot of mushy peas, a pool of bright red ketchup; bread and butter on a plate beside it and a glass of orange Fanta to go with it, which is a good drink to have with fish and chips. This was even better than the fish and chips in Scarborough, and that had been in my top three ever.

Uncle Universe watched me eat for a while.

"Right," he said eventually, as I chewed another large mouthful. "So first off, I was very sorry to hear you were ill, Jasper. I was going to come and see you soon. But based on what your mum's told me, I'm confident they can treat it and make you better."

I swallowed my mouthful a bit too quickly and had to pause a moment while it went down. "You were going to come and see me?" I asked.

"Of course I was!" he said. "You're my favourite nephew."

"I'm your only nephew," I muttered. It was a joke from when I was little.

Uncle Universe smiled. "It's high time me and your mum settled our differences," he told me. "Because I miss you. And her too, as it happens, but don't tell her that."

I stared at him. This was a bit too much to take in. "So I didn't even have to run away?"

Uncle Universe shrugged just a little bit. "Well," he said, "that's something I'm a tiny bit curious about. I'm overjoyed to see you, Jasper, I absolutely, positively am … but why did you come and find me?"

He had a mug of tea in front of him. He sipped it, waiting. I tapped my fork on my plate.

Tink, tink, tink.

It was a sharp, cross little noise.

"You know," I said, "how we used to call you Uncle Universe? Because your brain is as big as the universe?"

His lips moved. They pursed together like he was trying not to smile again. I didn't like him doing that, I felt like he might be laughing at me. I started again.

"So my parents, they're great in lots of ways, but they basically still treat me like a kid, and they want me to carry on as normal; but my life isn't normal any more, it's about as far from normal as it's possible to be!" I took a breath, trying to slow myself down. "And you're a doctor," I continued. "With a huge brain." I put down my fork, got

270

the letter out of my bag and tapped it. "And you literally said, in this letter, that if I ever needed you, I should come and find you." I took the letter out of the envelope, slapped it on the table in front of him and pointed at the sentence.

Anything you need, <u>absolutely anything</u>, please come to me. I'll help, I promise. Because I'm magic!

"Anything I need, absolutely anything. You underlined it! So I've come to see you because I need you to help me with the cancer. Which I've been calling Steve. And also with, you know, life. I want to live with you, for a while at least. Please."

That was it, I'd said everything I needed to say. I leant back. My hands were shaking a bit so I pressed them flat on the table. And I waited.

Uncle Universe nodded slowly. "Right," he murmured. He wasn't trying not to smile any more. In fact, his lips were a straight line now. He looked like Mrs Wells doing her stern/concerned face. His eyes were on the letter, reading it slowly. He sighed. "Right," he said again. "One or two things to unpack there."

I lifted my shaky hands off the table and squashed some chips into a piece of bread and butter. The chips were all salty and vinegary, and they made the butter melt. A chip butty on fluffy white bread is one of the nicest things ever, but I took a big bite and hardly tasted it. I didn't really know what he meant about unpacking things, but maybe that was just part of him being brilliant. I picked up my fork and tapped it on my plate again.

Tink, tink, tink.

And I waited to hear what he was going to say.

He looked up from the letter and met my nervous eyes with his kind eyes. "So first of all, I'm not a medical doctor," he said. "I'm a doctor of archaeology. Which means I do a bit of teaching and I go out on sites and dig things up. Sorry. And second of all, yes, my sister, your dear mother, used to call me Mr Universe when we were growing up, but it wasn't because my brain was as big as the universe. She said my *head* was as big as the universe."

He tapped his skull.

I swallowed my chips and bread. It felt like all the food was forming a solid, stodgy lump in my stomach.

"And third of all, living with me? That's a big step. That needs some discussion."

His eyes were on me and he was trying to smile at me, but he looked worried, as if he wasn't sure how I'd feel about what he was saying. He pushed his fingers through his hair, which made wisps of it stand up and made him look like a scientist. He looked at my hand, which was still tapping my fork on my plate.

Tink, tink, tink.

"You're not a doctor," I said finally, my voice flat, like all the feeling had drained out of it. "But you used to always be talking about skeletons..."

He raised his eyebrows. Small smile. "Archaeology."

So it turned out six-year-old me was a fool.

I stopped tapping. I was starting to feel angry now. All of a sudden, I was properly, tooth-grittingly, nostrils-flaringly, heart-thumpingly furious. I was furious with six-year-old me for getting it wrong about what the nickname Uncle Universe meant; furious with the doctor sitting in her office, telling me I had cancer; furious with my parents for **CARRY ON AS NORMAL!**; and furious with Uncle Universe, especially with him, for not being a proper doctor, and not being (somehow) the answer to all my problems. He was just Uncle Harvey, who was the answer to absolutely nothing.

"But you *promised*!" I told him, leaning forwards, almost shouting that last word at him. "'Just come to me and I'll help,' you said. 'Anything you need, anything at all,' you said. Well, I need to get better!"

People at other tables were looking at us. I didn't care. Uncle Universe laid his hand on mine. His eyes found mine and he nodded slowly. "This is so scary," he told me, like I didn't already know that, like I hadn't been scared ever since Thursday, when the doctor said what she said. "I'm so sorry you have to go through this. But I'm going to be with you, same as your parents, all the way."

"What does that even mean?" I snapped. I tried to keep the fury out of my voice, but I could hear it thrumming away in everything I said. My words sounded jagged and hostile, like they were a stick I was jabbing him with. I pulled my hand away from his.

"The very best people to help you, Jasper," Uncle Universe said gently, "the ones whose brains really are as big as the universe, are the brilliant cancer doctors and the brilliant nurses you're going to meet."

"Yeah," I muttered. "But not you."

I knew I wasn't being reasonable. Of course I knew that. It wasn't his fault if he couldn't live up to my completely unrealistic expectations. But I didn't care. He sat there with his irritating gentle voice, kind eyes, stern/concerned face and his childish Tardis T-shirt, sipping his tea like an old man, and he basically shrugged and told me that no, he couldn't help me. Sorry about that. He basically told me I'd come to Robin Hood's Bay for nothing, because he wasn't clever and he wasn't a doctor and the promise was a lie.

So the whole thing had been a complete waste of time.

And a complete waste of hope.

"Going to the loo," I said. It was quite hard to get the four words out, because my throat seemed to have closed up.

I stood up. The "going to the loo" trick had worked once before so I was doing it again. I didn't have any kind of plan; I just knew I needed to get away from him. There was a back door next to the loo this time, so I didn't have to climb out of the window. I opened the door and walked out.

THIRTY-TWO

A seagull was perched on a smelly bin. Grey wings, white chest, scary curved beak.

And yes, it definitely had claws.

I looked at the seagull and the seagull looked at me, cocking its head like it was asking if I was going to give it any trouble.

"No," I said. "You're fine."

I wanted to be that seagull. If I was that seagull I'd fly up into the sky, out over the sea, and I wouldn't have to worry about anything at all except catching a fish for my tea. It opened its beak and let out an angry squawk, which made me jump, then it hopped off the bin on to the ground and started pushing a greasy bit of chip paper around with its clawed black foot. I screwed up the letter I was still holding, screwed it up into a small ball, then lifted the lid of the bin, chucked the letter in and banged the lid down. The seagull squawked again and flew off.

I walked away.

I had no idea what I was doing. But really, right now, it felt like that had been true since Saturday morning when I'd got on the train to Scarborough. Or before that actually, ever since Thursday evening, on the roof in my garden. Or even before that, ever since I'd been in the doctor's office, looking over her shoulder at the scan on her screen, wondering what it meant. Her saying "malignant" and my mum starting to cry, my dad going white, and a lonely, scared feeling flooding into me.

I'd had no idea what I was doing ever since then. I hadn't been acting like a rational almost-adult with a sensible plan. I'd been lost, stumbling around, getting my friends into trouble, and just generally being unbelievably useless.

So, should I run to the station, jump on a train, hide in the loo and travel to London? Running had got me this far.

"Where are we going then, mate?"

It was Uncle Harvey. He was suddenly there next to me.

I jumped.

He raised his eyebrows. "I may not be brilliant, but I'm not a complete fool either. I guessed you were doing a runner. Would you like to come back to mine?"

"No!" I snapped at him.

"Jasper," he said, calm and patient, "I'm sorry I'm not what you hoped for. I really am. I wish I could snap my fingers and fix everything. I'm a disappointment, aren't I?"

"Yeah, you are," I snapped again.

He nodded, as if I'd said something sensible. "But I do know this," he said. "You can't just run away from your problems. When you try and do that, it turns out you just bring them with you."

"*You* ran away!" I was suddenly properly yelling at him. "I used to see you all the time, but then you weren't there any more, and Mum wouldn't say what had happened, you'd just gone, and all I had was that letter!"

I pointed at the bin.

He put a hand on my shoulder. "You're absolutely right," he said. "I did just go, I did run away, I did send you that ridiculous letter, and I'm extraordinarily sorry about every bit of that."

I shrugged the hand off my shoulder. "I don't need you," I told him.

He nodded again. "No, I don't think you do." He was looking right into my eyes again, which was a bit embarrassing, so I lowered mine, but he didn't stop talking.

"You don't need me because you've got your parents, and from what I hear you've got remarkable friends. And you've got yourself here without any help, which is impressive. And, by the way, you've also got the NHS, which is one of the most excellent things this country has ever done. So you're right: me with my PhD in archaeology and my promises I can't keep – I'm completely superfluous. But the thing is, Jasper, I'm your uncle, and I would very much like to be a part of your life. I can't cure you, but I can definitely support you. If you'll let me."

He was still looking right at me, and I was still looking at my trainers. Which were filthy.

He glanced over at the bin. "You put my letter in there?" he said.

I nodded, not trusting myself to speak.

"Best place for it," he told me. "I should never have promised I could help you. That's the sort of vague, meaningless claptrap grown-ups say without thinking about it. Here's what I should have said then, but I'm saying it now instead: you'll always be my favourite nephew, Jasper, and I'll always love you." He let out a slow breath, sounding sad. "I should have just said that."

I didn't know what to say to him then, but my chest was full and my lips were pressed tightly together and I realized I was holding my breath. I blew it out with an angry, puffy sound.

Uncle Harvey just waited, apparently not in any hurry.

"I was wondering about going to London," I said finally, in a small voice. "But actually, I think I want to phone my mum."

Uncle Harvey nodded slowly. "Good," he said. "Also – and this is important – I've got almond Magnums in the freezer at home."

278

THIRTY-THREE

He offered to call Mum for me, but I thought the rational, organized, grown-up choice was to take responsibility and do it myself. I kept it brief, apologized, said I'd see her at Uncle Harvey's. She was half an hour away.

We walked slowly back to his. I mean, we had to go slowly, because my legs still felt like they were full of porridge and there was that vertical hill to climb again. We didn't talk about anything serious the whole way. He told me about his job at Northumbria University, how his favourite thing was fieldwork, getting his hands dirty at a dig, uncovering layers of history. He said it was a bit like digging up stories. As we turned into Cliff Terrace he smiled when he saw a car outside his house.

"Nev's back," he said. "He's a nurse. You can ask him medical questions."

He opened the red front door and Nev came into the hall.

"Ah-ha," he boomed, too loud, too hearty. "This must be Jasper. Good to meet you, dude."

Uncle Harvey winced and looked at me. "Nev's not used to talking to teenagers," he said.

"Hi," I said to Nev. I quite liked being called "dude".

We sat in the room with the big TV and the stove, and I ate an almond Magnum. My favourite is the caramel one, but almond is all right too. This was nothing like Dottie's lounge, and it was nothing like the TV room in my house. That always has video games and controllers lying around, usually a couple of mugs and maybe a plate or two, some crumbs on the coffee table, and quite often a stray pea on the floor. There was no mess at all in this room: the sofa was all soft and comfortable and the not-quite-white colour of white chocolate. I had my hand cupped under my Magnum, being careful not to drop any bits on the floor.

"You walked here?" Nev said. "You walked, mostly on your own, all the way from Scarborough? Mate, respect."

I liked Nev. He was a bit younger than Uncle Harvey, with very dark skin, and he had a big smile like he thought I was hilarious, even though I hadn't said anything funny. He was wearing his nurse's uniform: pale blue trousers and a pale blue top, and he ate his whole Magnum in two bites, which impressed me. Now he'd stopped with the patronizing voice, he was mostly talking to me like I was his age. I told them both about the caravan full of dogs.

"I mean, *full* of dogs," I said. "And when he opened the

door I threw a dog in his face, and then a whole river of dogs came pouring out. It was a **DOG EXPLOSION!**" I said it loud, throwing my hands in the air, so they'd know it needed big, capital letters and an exclamation mark.

They were both laughing. "You threw a dog in his face?" Nev cackled. "Of course you did! Wish I'd met you sooner, Jasper." He pointed at Uncle Harvey. "I told him not to fall out with his family."

We both looked at him.

"Why did you?" I asked.

They'd stopped laughing.

Uncle Harvey sighed. "It was issues around your grandmother's will. It felt huge at the time, but now … not so much. Maybe we can get past it. And if we do, it'll be because of you Jasper, coming all this way to see me. It makes our whole argument feel fatuous, to be quite honest."

"Been telling him that for years," Nev said.

I wasn't sure what "fatuous" meant, but I nodded like I understood.

"I fell out with one of my friends," I said. "I thought it couldn't be fixed – thought it had gone beyond talking. But I was wrong about that. It's probably always worth trying, isn't it?"

Nev pointed at me and grinned and nodded. "This guy," he said. He didn't say anything else, just went to the kitchen.

Uncle Harvey finished his Magnum and tapped the stick on his palm. "So, I'll say one more thing," he told me, "if that's all right. I'm sure you've noticed that adults are just awash with issues and problems. Which means you have every right to be disappointed with me and with all the other adults who can't help you, who just hover around being awkward and irritating."

He broke the stick, and looked down at it, surprised. "See?" he said. "Awkward. But I suppose the one bit of advice I'd give you is: don't turn away from it, Jasper. Call it Steve if it helps, and sure, skip school now and then, and come and see me and Nev whenever you want, but I think you need to accept that that nasty little tumour is in there." He was pointing vaguely towards my right shoulder. "You're going to feel strange for a while, people around you are going to be downright weird sometimes, and your life will be" – he paused – "different."

I nodded, not looking at him. I didn't want my life to be different, but it was going to happen anyway. That's why **CARRY ON AS NORMAL!** made no sense.

He smiled at me as if he felt like we'd got to the end of a difficult conversation. He checked the time on his phone. "Your mum and dad will be here any minute," he said.

I finished my Magnum and looked at the stick. I didn't feel like we'd got to the end of our conversation. Not yet. There was something that I hadn't talked about with my parents because, in spite of what I'd just said about it always being worth trying, I wasn't sure I *could* talk about it with them.

I glanced back at Uncle Harvey. "You must see, I guess ... lots of dead stuff ... with your work?" My words stumbled out, slow and hesitant.

His eyes were on me again, as if he was watching the thoughts moving through my brain. "Sure," he said. "Anglo-Saxon lords with their treasure and their weapons, ordinary people, pets. Fascinating how funeral rituals change over the centuries."

He paused, and when I didn't reply he said, "I expect death's been on your mind, Jasper?"

Option Three. The toad squatting inside my head. The feeling I'd had near the caravan, that my life might just ... stop. I nodded. I didn't feel like speaking.

"So Nev says the treatment won't be much fun," Uncle Harvey told me, "but it's effective. And the cancer hasn't spread, which is good news. They're going to zap it with chemo, cut it out and get rid of it."

I was staring at my hands, and I didn't look up. "So you think I'll get better?" It came out as not much more than a whisper, but the room was quiet and I'm sure he heard.

Uncle Harvey breathed in deep and breathed out slowly. "I'm no expert, Jasper, but I want to always be honest with you. So I'm going to say yes. Probably."

I looked up at him, surprised. That wasn't quite what I wanted to hear. "You don't sound very sure."

He smiled. "Will I be alive and well this time tomorrow?" He shrugged. "Probably. I reckon 'probably' is as good as it gets, Jasper, for any of us. I reckon you can take 'probably' and run with it."

I nodded slowly. Neither of us said anything for about ten seconds. Uncle Harvey checked the time again.

"Before your folks get here," he said, "we should talk about what you said before. About living with me."

I looked at him. Hair spilling down to his collar, long face, big nose, Mum's eyes. He was looking back at me, curious and concerned, probably wondering how to let me down gently. I was thinking about my friends. Suravi in the flat: "We're not going to just leave you here." Barney in the woods: "We're OK with getting into trouble. We just want to help you." Maika on the Cleveland Way: "We have to support him, that's what friends do." And I remembered how I'd felt when they found me in the woods, near the caravan. That rush of gratitude, that sudden feeling of ... well ... love.

I looked down at my Magnum stick. I wasn't sure what to do with it. There was the sound of a car outside and Uncle Harvey looked out of the window.

"That's your parents doing a nifty bit of parallel parking."

When I heard that, I realized how happy I was to see them, even though they were going to be furious and embarrassingly emotional and desperate to interrogate me. Perhaps *because* of those things.

"Don't worry," I said. "I don't want to move in with you. That was just an idea. A bad idea. No offence."

284

He laughed. "None taken."

I really liked Uncle Harvey, and Nev seemed nice, but of course I didn't want to move in with them. I wanted to stay at home with my parents and my friends. He was getting up, but I stopped him. "Wait," I said. There was one more thing I wanted to ask him. He sat down again.

"That story you used to tell me," I said. "It was in a little village called Oswaldhover, and it was about a boy called Jasper…"

He laughed. "I remember that! Someone turned up in a boat in the sky and kidnapped him, right?"

I nodded. "Yes, that's it. And he jumped out of the boat and escaped. But I was trying to remember what happened after that."

There was a loud, urgent KNOCK! KNOCK! KNOCK! at the front door. We both jumped, and Uncle Harvey shifted as if he wanted to get up.

"Wait, tell me what happens next!" I said. "What happens after he jumps out of the boat?"

Uncle Harvey's eyes glazed a bit, as he tried to remember that story, which he probably hadn't thought about for nine years. He shook his head eventually. "I don't know," he said. Nev was coming out of the kitchen, into the hall. "Don't know." He lifted his shoulders in a shrug. "I was making it up as I went along. And you helped me, do you remember?"

I nodded slowly. It was starting to come back to me. I'd told him things I wanted to have happen in the story.

"I think it's actually your story, Jasper, not mine," Uncle Harvey told me. "So in fact, what happens next is up to you."

Nev opened the front door.

TUESDAY, WEDNESDAY, THURSDAY

THIRTY-FOUR

On Tuesday, Mum and Dad took the day off and we had a pub lunch out on the moor.

I realized after a minute that they weren't eating. They were just sitting there, staring at me.

I swallowed most of a mouthful of lasagne. "What?" I said.

"We're sorry," Mum said.

I shook my head, which nearly made pasta spill out of my mouth. "No, I'm sorry! I shouldn't have run away."

Dad put his hands up, palms outwards. "You don't have to apologize any more."

Mum picked up a chip and looked at it for a moment, then looked at me. "We were wrong about carrying on as normal," she said thoughtfully, "and we'll probably be wrong again soon, maybe lots of times, because this is all new. But the important thing," she wagged the chip at me, "is saying what we're feeling."

Dad nodded, picking up his burger. He's not very good at just sitting there when there's food in front of him. "Lines of communication," he said, and then he took an enormous bite and ketchup squirted out.

I'd been apologizing pretty much constantly since they'd walked into Uncle Harvey's house on Monday. One more time couldn't hurt.

"OK," I said, "but I really am sorry."

"Well, yes," said Mum, with a small smile. "You did frighten the life out of us. So, from now on, whatever's on your mind, we talk about it. That's the rule. Right?"

She finally ate the chip she was holding.

"Yes," I said. It wasn't quite that simple. There were still things it was easier to talk about with other people, but I agreed with the general principle.

After lunch we had a walk round the reservoir, which was all right if you like that sort of thing. I mean, it wasn't the Cleveland Way, but Dad heard a curlew, which pleased him.

On Wednesday we saw the nurse, who told me pretty much exactly what Nev and Uncle Harvey had told me: that the treatment won't be much fun but they think it'll be effective. She explained about limb-sparing surgery, which they hope will mean I won't lose my arm. We were back in the realm of "probably", which was fair enough, because the answer was in the future, in the next few weeks and months. She said a lot more about the treatment which I didn't really understand, but I got to see the ward, which had an Xbox in the common room. The nurse had a bit of a soppy smile and a soft voice, talking to me as if I was made of glass and I might break, but she was all right. The hospital smelled like school meals and soap, and it had corridors that seemed to go on literally for ever. I didn't like it. Apart from the Xbox.

When we got home, no one really knew what to say. I felt like I still had the smell of the hospital in my nostrils.

Anyway, now it's Thursday, and I'm picking at the black material on the shed roof again. The sky's grey, like my white T-shirt that's been in the coloured wash too many times. I can smell autumn – damp earth, cut grass, a wisp of woodsmoke.

I sit up, careful not to slide off the roof, scrunch my eyes and look down the garden. I'm looking for Suravi, Maika and Barney, but there's no sign of them. I thought they would've been here by now. It's after five o'clock, so school's been finished for a while. I lie back down again.

Treatment starts tomorrow. Chemotherapy. And we're having fish for tea today because the fish man is in the market on Thursdays. Dad's cooking, and it's not fish and chips, it's fish curry, which I doubt will make my top ten favourite meals but I won't tell him that. It's going to make me feel sick, apparently. (The chemo, not the fish curry.) And my hair will probably fall out. (Because of the chemo, not the curry.)

I drum my fingernails on the roof, on the bare patch where I've picked away the black stuff. The nurse said she and the doctors were optimistic, but I'm having trouble feeling that way to be honest. I'm hoping for the best, but that's not the same thing. And where are Barney, Suravi and Maika? We haven't actually talked about it, but surely they're going to come and see me on the day before my treatment starts? But maybe not. Maybe they aren't coming. Maybe their parents have told them to stay away because I'm a bad influence. Which is fair. I did, in fact, get them all picked up by the police. Maybe they're annoyed with me because I abandoned them in Scarborough and then told them I was going to stay in Robin Hood's Bay.

A high-pitched wail cuts through the silence then turns into a *Wah wah wah*.

I flinch and nearly fall right off the roof, which takes me back to nearly falling off the roof in Scarborough and makes my heart jump in my chest.

I sit up again. "I nearly fell off the roof!" I yell.

I try to sound cross but I don't sound cross at all because the wail was Barney's harmonica, and here they all are at last: Maika, Suravi, Barney and Milo. Of course they've come. They're my best friends.

I haven't seen Maika since Robin Hood's Bay so we haven't had another kiss yet, but that's a thing that might happen. Let's call it Option Four – me and Maika.

Milo is barking at me, wagging his tail and straining

at his lead. So I do slide off the roof at this point, but on purpose. It's OK – if you get to the edge and just hang down, you're only a couple of feet off the ground.

Barney and Suravi have brought a trestle table and they start trying to put it up. Maika has a couple of camping chairs under each arm. She drops them and starts unfolding them. I'm sort of squinting at my friends and rubbing my forehead at this point.

"OK," I say, "what you doing?"

"What's it look like, genius?" says Suravi.

Barney grins. "We're having tea in your garden!"

"Are we?" I say. It's news to me.

"Our parents too," says Maika.

"And your uncle's shown up with someone called Nev," Suravi says.

"He called me 'dude'," Barney tells me, proudly.

I nod. "He does that." I look at them all, suddenly in my garden with a table and chairs, like it's normal. "I didn't know this was happening."

"No," says Maika. "It's a surprise."

"Surprise!" shouts Barney, making me jump.

"You OK?" says Suravi.

"Well," I say. "Still got cancer."

"Yeah, apart from that!" Suravi replies, smiling. We sit down on the camping chairs. I've been feeling a bit rubbish because of the smelly hospital with the endless corridors, because of chemotherapy starting tomorrow and because

293

of fish curry for tea, but now my friends are here, and that helps.

"Yeah," I tell Suravi. "I'm OK. Are you getting kicked out of school, though? Have you heard what's happening?"

"I'm on a final warning," she says, smiling as if that's a good thing. "And that cow got in trouble for calling me 'Subaru'."

I nod. "Good." I look at Barney. "I'm sorry I haven't been there to help with Joe Hancock."

Barney shrugs.

"We're there," says Maika.

"And you will be soon," says Suravi.

"And I can take care of myself," says Barney.

He doesn't sound too sure about that, and I don't feel too sure about it either, but he was definitely brave in Robin Hood's Bay. And Suravi controlled her temper with Dottie, Maika got rid of the last of her Barbies, Barney and Suravi seem like they're OK with each other. It's not perfect. I'm not sure that Uncle Harvey and my mum are proper friends yet, and even if I feel like I can cope with Steve now, and can talk about it when I need to, Options Two and Three are still there, dangling ahead of me.

But I can't change that, so I prefer to focus on better things, because Option Four is there too, me and Maika, and – probably – Option Five, which is growing up. The whole unknowable future. I choose to believe in those things. So life may not be perfect right now, but that's OK, because the truth is, perfect is impossible.

"I guess," I say, sighing, "that we never found a Perfect Moment, did we?"

"Yes, we did," Barney says immediately, his voice firm and certain.

I shake my head. "No, I don't think perfect is even possible," I tell him.

"Of course it is, you muppet," Suravi says.

"We were talking about it on the way over," Maika tells me.

"From when we met at Maika's on Saturday," Suravi says, explaining it slowly and clearly, as if I might not understand, "right through to when the police showed up at Dottie's house, that was one long Perfect Moment. Trust me," she says, nodding, tapping her chest. "I'm always right."

"And our Moment lasted even longer," Maika says. She's looking at me, smiling.

I nod slowly, looking back at her. "I remember."

"It was all of it!" Barney says. "The whole thing was one big Perfect Moment!" And Milo barks his agreement.

I'm not sure what to say to that, I just start smiling too, a wide smile that smears right across my face and includes all three of them.

And then a whole crowd comes out of the house. Dad's carrying a great big saucepan, chatting to Nev, and

Mum has a load of naans and poppadums and is talking to Uncle Harvey, who's carrying plates, and behind them are Maika's mum and Barney and Suravi's parents, who have more chairs and glasses and bottles and cutlery.

And the fish curry is actually pretty good, I love naan bread and poppadums, and Dad gives me a cold beer to mark the occasion, and that whole tea definitely goes straight to the top of my list of best teas ever.

And I can't stop looking over at Maika.

And maybe I don't know what's in the future, but I think I'll be able to deal with it because of all the people who are in this garden with me.

Halfway through the meal, Suravi's mother says she has no idea where her daughter gets her temper from, and her dad stares at Suravi and says, "You're going to mend your ways, aren't you?" Suravi rolls her eyes and nods and mumbles yes, but then, when no one's looking at us, she leans in close to me and whispers a question. Her mouth is really full so the words are muffled, but I can just about make out what she's saying.

She says: "Where are we going to run away to next?"

ACKNOWLEDGEMENTS

First of all, huge thanks to Florence for her very useful comments and her fantastic mind-map, and to her mum Rebecca for her encouragement and her lovely comments. I'd also like to thank the wonderful Phil Earle, who gave me great advice and support. If you haven't read his work, you really should, he's brilliant. Thanks also to Melvin Burgess (another brilliant writer, of course) and Ben Jancovich. I'm very grateful for the weekly walks and coffees, which unravel stress and make me feel larger (not literally). And thanks to Holly and Sam, who are inspiring in more ways than one.

Many thanks to Jo Unwin for liking this book, for continuing to support me in dry periods, for a couple of excellent suggestions that made a significant difference, and for seeing it on its way to Charlotte Colwill. Thanks to Charlotte for all her work, especially her notes, which definitely made it a better book. Thanks to Ian Eagleton, for his particular point of view, which was very helpful, and thanks to all at Scholastic, for all their hard work, suggestions and enthusiasm, especially Tierney Holm and Linas Alsenas.

Thanks to Sal for most of the things I've mentioned above (including excellent notes but not including the mind-map) and so much more. I mean, *so* much more.

Thanks to the Royal Literary Fund, who have supported thousands of writers over the centuries and I'm proud to be one of them. Thanks also to York St John University and York University where I worked for the RLF and where I got to know York, which has a starring role in this book. And I'd like to mention the Raven Hall Hotel, near Robin Hood's Bay, where I've had excellent stays, and where I've never stolen a breakfast.

My love and thanks to friends and family who were so important back when I was a teenager, going through something similar to Jasper – my parents and my brother, Dean, and Rich, Rob, Heather, Di, Jonny, Mark, and the late, much-missed, Phil Selby. And thank you to Alan Horwich, Jacqui Greenwood and Ginny Mildred, a doctor, nurse and physio who I dedicated my first novel to, way back in 1988, and who I've dedicated this one to as well.

Beyond those three individuals, I'd like to finally offer heartfelt thanks to the NHS as a whole. The extent to which we properly fund, safeguard, and cherish it is a measure of how civilized we are.